Croissants, Crimes & Canines

Book 9 in
The New Orleans Go Cup Chronicles

Colleen Mooney

Dedication

To all my fans who love reading my work,
thank you!

Chapter One

Friday 5:30 p.m.

"WOW, WHAT A first week," Ava said pulling her fiery red hair into a scrunchie as I drove her to look at an apartment she might rent. "I love the job, and I like Julia and Frank, but I have to get out of their bed and breakfast. Those two are constantly screaming at each other. I can't make out what they are saying because the masks muffle their voices."

"They feed off each other," I said, "if you haven't noticed."

"Brandy, I know we're in a pandemic, but Frank is sanitizing everything over and over. He's literally wiping down whatever I touch as my hand is leaving the surface," she said.

"Frank and Julia are fanatical, both in screaming and in cleaning," I said. "I didn't plan on you being there long, only a couple of days. I can move you to a hotel."

"I don't want to sound ungrateful," Ava said putting her hand to her heart.

"No, I'm more concerned you'll hate me forever for

making your reservation there," I said laughing. "New job, new place, in a new city is a challenge."

"Even though I grew up here, a lot has changed since I left here for college," Ava said. "We had just finished high school, so I don't remember as much as I thought. I appreciate you helping me find a nice place in a nice neighborhood."

"Jiff and I have been looking at homes to buy. It's frustrating, not to mention, time consuming. Plus, we still must pick a date and a place for us to get married," I said.

"I thought you set the date," she said.

"We did. It was this past November….but that's a story that involves cocktails – several cocktails," I said shaking my head. "Now with the pandemic, we're thinking we'll forgo the wedding reception and get his mother to marry us." I stole a quick look at Ava taking my eyes off the road for a second. "She's a judge. His family is super nice…the total opposite of mine. I feel like I'm winning the husband and in-law lottery. I never wanted the big to-do wedding and reception, just something meaningful for the two of us."

"Sounds like an interesting guy you found there," she said looking from her notepad to the house addresses as I crawled up the street this apartment was supposed to be in.

"I don't know about this neighborhood," I said looking around trying to spot the house address. "Since you left, many neighborhoods have changed…for the worse."

"If you don't think it's safe, let's not get out of the car," she said.

I stopped at the curb in front of a double, one among many, along the street.

"These houses all look like someone used a cookie cutter to make them," Ava said. "All these houses look alike. They're even painted the same color."

All were built about the same period with a divided front porch, entry door on each side in the front and a driveway along each side. Usually there was a divided yard in the back, so each side had part of it to use.

"I wonder how often someone comes home after a few too many and tries the wrong door," I said. "Here it is. Are you sure this is the right address?"

"It looks like the New York neighborhood I lived in right after college," she said wrinkling her nose. "When my dad saw it, he said, 'You should ask Santa for a bullet proof vest...and wear it'."

I smiled thinking of her dad as I turned off the ignition. When I looked up, I noticed there was a late-model, red Camaro parked two houses in front of me. I could see exhaust coming out of the tailpipe and no one in the car. *I thought, who would leave a nice car like that running in this neighborhood?*

Just then, before we decided to get out or pull away, we heard what sounded like a gunshot.

"Was that...." Ava grabbed my hand as she asked me, her eyes wide.

"I think so," I said looking around for anyone brandishing a weapon.

"Where did it come from?" Ava asked scanning the area in front and behind the car.

"That house where that red Camaro is parked, I think." I pushed her down onto the seat just as three more shots were fired. I could hear my heart beating loudly in my ears.

As I pulled myself together to peek over the dashboard, I saw two men wearing dark hoodies and jeans run out of the house where the Camaro was parked with a very big dog chasing them. The dog looked like a giant Schnauzer and he leaped forward to grab one guy's arm. Unfortunately, he was the guy with the gun who was trying to get in on the passenger side. When the dog grabbed his right arm without the gun, the guy fired a shot, hitting the dog who let go and fell to the ground.

The one who ran to the driver's side of the car looked around as he jumped in behind the wheel.

"Stay down!" I said to Ava. I really hoped neither guy saw us or paid attention to my BMW parked few car lengths behind them. I heard tires screeching as they took off. I hit Ava on the arm and said, "Let's go!" as I started to get out of the car. I had to pry my arm out of the grip she still held on me.

"Let's go? I thought you meant, let's go as in, let's get out of here, not let's get out of the car," she said running to catch up. "It feels like we should stay in the car."

"We *definitely* should stay in the car, but that dog just got shot trying to stop those two. Ava, c'mon, we need to see if we can help him."

When I got to the dog, I bent down, and saw he was still alive. He seemed in shock as he didn't try to bite me. The bullet looked like it went through his chest. I took off a silk scarf and rolled it long and skinny. Then I tied it around the dog's mouth to muzzle him in case he came to or reacted violently trying to bite someone, namely, me. Next, I used my suit jacket to try and stop the bleeding.

"Quick, call 911 and give them this address," I said applying pressure to the dog's wound. He didn't try to bite me, so I thought he was unconscious. "There might be people inside who are injured or dead."

Ava ran inside to look.

"Ava, no!" I yelled at her as she disappeared into the house. "Call 911!" I yelled louder. I hoped whoever was shot in there didn't have a gun aimed at the front door waiting for someone to come back.

I could hear her inside shouting, "Is anyone in here hurt or need help? Call out!"

I didn't hear anyone except Ava. She rushed back out making a call on her cell as she made her way over to me and the dog.

"I saw a man and a woman, both shot. I'm pretty sure he's dead. The woman is moaning but she's alive," she said to me. Then, into her cell phone she gave the address, nature of the issue and asked them to send an ambulance.

"Here, Ava, can you pull my car up to here and then help me get this big guy in my back seat. We're taking him to a vet." I looked at my watch, and it was only 5:50 pm. My vet was still at his clinic until 8:00 p.m.

"I need to wait here with that woman," Ava said.

"Not a good idea," I said applying pressure to the wounds on this giant dog that could take my face off if he came to.

"I'm staying. I lived in New York, remember?" She said over her shoulder as she ran to move my car up to where the dog was lying on the front lawn.

"Did you see what just happened? Look, they might come back if one of them remembers seeing me parked behind them," I said.

"There's a couple inside who were shot. The woman, is still alive. She might make it," she said.

"Okay, I'll call someone I know in homicide on my way to the vet. I'll ask them to send someone here, asap," I said while Ava and I huffed and puffed struggling to get Volker—the name on his tag-across the back seat before jumping behind the wheel. "You're sure you want to stay?"

"If it was me in there, I'd want someone to wait with me."

"I'll call Dante on my way. He's Captain of Homicide in New Orleans now. I'll get back here as soon as I can. I put the car in drive and screeched away from the curb.

Chapter Two

M Y NAME IS Brandy Alexander, and no, I'm not a stripper. Many people guess that's why I have a rapport with the police—from a working girl association. It's really because I grew up next door to Dante Deedler, my childhood sweetheart and now Captain of the New Orleans Homicide Division. I live in New Orleans and my name is wasted on me and my rather boring job with a large telecom company. I work investigating fraud and phone scams for the biggest customers in the state.

I felt around in my purse for my cell phone while keeping my eyes on where I was heading while driving way too fast.

I asked Siri, "Call Dante Deedler."

"Is that Captain Dante Deedler or Dante or do you want Dante Deedler?" Siri asked.

"They are all the same. Just call the number," I said.

"Do you want his mobile, office or home?" asked Siri.

"For God's sake, Siri. He doesn't have a home number. Cell! Call the cell!" I lost my patience with Siri every time I had to deal with her. It made me wonder why I just didn't dial it myself. I could have been talking to him by now.

Dante and I had been an item since birth, mainly because we lived next door to each other. Both sets of parents wanted us married off—to each other. Dante didn't get the memo. Then, I met and kissed a guy in front of everyone …both sets of parents and Dante…at a Mardi Gras parade. The guy I kissed, I was now engaged to and trying to keep the wedding secret from my mother until all the plans were made. Dante and I were working on mending our fence, i.e. the split-up of our relationship which, in my opinion, never really got off the ground.

I drove as fast as I could while trying not to hit anyone or run any lights. I wasn't sure how long the Giant Schnauzer had left in him.

"Deedler. Homicide."

"Dante, it's me, why are you answering your phone like you're at work? I expected Detective Hanky since she's relieving you. Aren't you supposed to be home for another week?" I asked.

Dante had just been released, a week ago, from the hospital due to an injury he sustained while in the line of duty. Doctors put him in a medically induced coma to keep his brain from swelling.

"I stayed at my mother's house for a week, and I

decided to chance it coming back to work. The stress of having my mother wake me up every fifteen minutes to see if I was all right is far greater than anything I have to deal with here."

"I hate to be the one to call you on your first day back on the job, but…"

"Then, hang up and call back tomorrow," he said. "Just kidding. Whatcha got?"

"There's been a shooting on Cambronne Street, right off Carrollton and Claiborne Avenue, you know where…"

"What are you doing in that neighborhood?" Dante cut me off.

"You remember, Ava? From grade school?" When he paused and I didn't know if he was thinking of something else or trying to remember I added, "Ava Frost. Cute, redhead, moved to New York…ringing any bells?"

"Oh yeah, a little anti-social, right?"

"She kept to herself," I answered him. "Anyway, she's moving back to New Orleans, and I'm helping her look for an apartment. When she gave me the address, I thought it was on the other side of Claiborne. I didn't realize where it was, exactly. After the gunmen left, she went into the house…"

"Gunmen? You went into a house with gunmen?" he screamed into the phone causing me to hold it at arm's length away from my ear. Even at this distance from my head I could hear him say, "With gunmen shooting?"

"I just said we saw the gunmen leave. We didn't go in while they were there. She went in. I didn't. You know, I bet the hospital told you not to let things stress you out when they released you. It sounds like you're getting stressed. Maybe I should talk to Hanky or Taylor?" I asked.

"I'm. Not. Stressed," he spoke slowly letting out an exhale you could hear all the way to the Louisiana/Texas state line. "Go on," he said in a forced relaxed tone, although I heard him snapping his fingers at someone to get his or her attention, probably to get cars rolling to the crime scene.

"We saw two guys leave. Both had guns, and the one getting in on the passenger side of the car shot the dog. I did see that. After they left, I went to help the dog, and Ava went into the house. She told me she saw two bodies. I'm taking the dog to the vet on Magazine Street as we speak. I'm almost there," I said in one breath as fast as I could so he couldn't cut me off again.

"I'm going back to the scene after I drop the dog. And, oh, the license plate on the red Camaro with the two gunmen fleeing the scene is a vanity plate, 'All Mine'. I must say, these two gangbangers can't be too smart to drive around in a car with a high vis license plate, so it's likely a stolen car."

"Yeah, it is. I'm looking at the BOLO on it. The owner said he was held at gunpoint at a drug store near where you saw them. Two guys wearing masks stole it.

A BOLO was put out almost an hour ago. Did you call an ambulance or 911?" he asked, and I could hear his chair scraping across the tile floor in his office as I imagined him jumping up out of it.

"Yes, Ava did. She stayed at thc house to wait with the woman who was moaning, not dead. She said the husband or man looked dead. She went in while I tried to help the dog, but I don't think she touched anything."

"It's a good thing they didn't have a gun pointed at the door waiting for the perps to come back," he said. "I'll be there. Go back to the crime scene after you take the dog to the vet so you can give us a statement."

Then he hung up in true 'Dante-style'. He never learned or practiced good phone etiquette. He didn't wait to hear I had to go back to pick up Ava anyway.

The next call I made was to my vet, and I said it was an emergency as soon as someone answered. I gave Kelly, the receptionist I know who answered the phone, the situation, telling her the dog was a Giant Schnauzer and it took two of us to get him into my car. I told her he seemed unconscious and asked if a tech could meet me in the back of the clinic. There was a back door there that didn't require going up steps. She said she would be out there to meet me with a stretcher for the dog with any of the vets who were free. I suggested they bring a muzzle, a real one, in case he came to. He's a big dog.

Kelly was with Dr. Scott and Dr. Kevin, two of the

vets waiting for me when I pulled up. They had a stretcher, and they did a quick look at him in my back seat and put the muzzle on him. "I'm guessing this is a rescue?" Dr. Scott asked as he moved to take some vitals on the dog.

"He is now," I said. "One owner is dead, and I'm not sure if the other one might be by the time I get back. I'll take him into my rescue and find him a home."

"Pretty good muzzle you did there on the fly. That was the right thing to do. He's big and he doesn't know you," Dr. Kevin said. "He looks to be about one hundred twenty pounds. How did you ever get him into your car?"

"He's really heavy," Dr. Scott said as the two men managed to get Volker out of the back seat of my BMW. "How did you get him in here all by yourself?"

"I had help, but I think adrenalin did most of the work," I said. "He's a brave dog. He tried to stop the men with guns who shot his owners and then shot him."

"His name, Volker, in German means guard of the people," Dr. Kevin said in his German tinged accent over his shoulder as he and Dr. Scott managed the weight of the dog onto a stretcher.

"I'll be back, and I'll pay for whatever he needs," I said to their backs as another vet tech ran up to help them with Volker by holding the rear door open.

I felt an overwhelming weight in my chest as tears

rolled down my cheeks when the door closed behind them. I realized I might not see this brave dog again. I said a prayer to St. Frances, patron saint of animals, to look over him and help him heal.

"Are you all right?" Kelly asked as she turned to follow the stretcher back inside the clinic.

"I will be when that dog makes it. I need to get back to the scene of that shooting. The police want me to make a statement."

Kelly stopped in her tracks and reeled around to ask, "Do you really need to go back there? That can't be safe."

"Yeah, I do. I left my friend there waiting for an ambulance with a woman who was shot but still alive…who might make it. I'll be fine, by the time I get back there the street will be crawling with police," I said sliding behind the wheel.

"Please be careful," she said as she waved goodbye.

Chapter Three

MY SOFT SPOT is abandoned dogs, particularly Schnauzers. After the fifth Schnauzer came my way—I already had taken in three and with Meaux that made four—so, I decided to join a rescue group that was breed specific. They only took in Schnauzers and found them forever homes. This is my way of giving back along with helping the police solve crimes I happen to witness. Abandoned or homeless Schnauzers and crime scenes find me. I don't go looking for them. Well, Schnauzers I look for.

The dogs always appreciate me. The police, however, never do.

I called my fiancé, Jiff, on the way back to the scene. He has a Schnauzer named Isabella. The first time I met him, well the second time, really, I went to meet him at the end of a parade after we kissed in the street. I saw him get shot and he asked me to 'save Isabella' before he was hauled away in an ambulance. I thought Isabella was his wife or girlfriend, but I felt it might be his dying wish, so I did my duty and was rewarded a hundred-fold for it.

I credit my rescue work as the reason we were cosmically attracted to each other. Jiff had seen me bring a rescued Schnauzer to a man who worked as security in the building where he lived. I found out later, he knew who I was, but I had never seen him.

When I told him what had happened while looking for an apartment for Ava, he asked, "Why does she want to live there? That's not the safest neighborhood for a single woman."

Wow, I thought, Dante said almost the exact same thing. "It's near the nursing home her dad is in, but I didn't realize which side of Claiborne it was on," I told him. "There was a dog, a Giant Schnauzer shot, along with two people that we know of. I just took him to my vet on Magazine Street. He was still alive when I got him there. I hope Dr. Scott can save him."

"If anyone can, they can. I'll have a good thought for him," Jiff said. "Call me when you two finish with your statements, and I'll take you to dinner. I'm sure you and Ava could use a little de-stressing."

"Deal. I'll let you know as soon as we are finished. Let me run. I just thought of something I want to tell the vet," I said. "Bye for now. Love you. Muah!" I always ended my calls with Jiff with the sound of sending him a big kiss. He always said he loved me and usually texted xoxo as his signature at the end of a call.

The next call I made was to the vet's office to ask if Kelly could get a message to Doctors Scott and Kevin working on Volker.

"Sure, what do you want me to tell them?" she asked.

"Ask them to take any hair that has blood on it and put it in a Ziplock. Also, if there's anything in the dog's teeth, please ask them to look and please put that in another Ziplock. I saw that dog bite the shooter, and he might have DNA in his teeth or on his face," I said.

"I'll give them the message ASAP. They probably were going to do that anyway since a gunshot was involved. We must call Animal Control who will notify the police. They are still working on him, but I'll call you, or Dr. Scott will, when they are finished to give you an update," Kelly said.

"Whoever contacts Animal Control, ask them to contact Captain Dante Deedler in Homicide who is working this case," I asked. I gave her his cell phone number.

"Sure thing," Kelly said.

"Thank you. You're the best," I said and hung up.

DETECTIVES TRAVIS TAYLOR and Zide Hanky were already on the scene when I returned. I had to park a block away since there were dozens of police cars, an ambulance, forensics' vehicles and unmarked cars covered the street like litter, broken beads, beer cans and plastic drink cups left after a Mardi Gras parade. As I walked up, I put on my mask.

Hanky spotted me and came charging up demanding through the mask she was wearing, "Did you have to call him on his first day back at work after being released from the hospital?" I could still see her eyes and they weren't sending friendly vibes.

"I thought you would answer. I thought you would still be relieving him," I said leaning back away from Hanky crowding my personal space. When she didn't answer or move back, I added, "I didn't shoot the two people in there or choreograph this hit, so would you rather for me to have ignored it all and call it in tomorrow?" I asked.

Hanky and I had relationship that is best described as "frienemy", you know friends, but enemies, at the same time. This started the instant we met when she became Dante's partner. Now that he was Captain of the Homicide Division, and she was partners with Detective Taylor, our relationship had improved a little. I think.

"Good one," she said. "Why did you leave the scene?"

"Well, one gunman shot a Giant Schnauzer out here on the lawn as the two suspects were fleeing. We saw it happen. I saw the dog chase them out of the house and grab one on the arm. The guy shot the dog with a handgun," I said. "I rushed him to my vet on Magazine. You know the one."

"Oh no!" Hanky said. "I'll shoot these gangbangers myself when we catch them for hurting that dog. They better hope he lives."

As tough a cop as Hanky was, she had a BIG soft spot for dogs and had even adopted one of my rescued mini-Schnauzers. She was less caustic toward me when a dog was involved. That's why I thought our relationship was improving, but I could be interpreting that all wrong.

She carried dog treats in her squad car to make friends with dogs at scenes and even had a vet prescribed tranquilizer in a pill pocket she'd give them so they wouldn't attack her when she encountered a vicious animal. Once she admitted to me that she could never shoot an animal. People, however, I believe she could use for target practice.

"Where's the woman who went inside to help? She called 911 and asked them to send an ambulance. She thought the guy looked dead, but the woman was moaning," I said.

"Two women were inside when I got here. One was shot in the shoulder. She wasn't dead, but she's in a bad way. The other one, a redhead, looked like she missed catching a bullet. She was administering comfort to the injured. The EMS people asked the one who wasn't shot to ride in the ambulance with the injured woman. Seems the victim grabbed the other one's arm and wouldn't let go. She lost a lot of blood," Hanky said. "I hope she can hold on until we question her."

"Did they go to University Medical Center?" I asked. "I'm guessing that's where they're taking gunshot victims these days?"

"Yeah, that's where they're going. The man in there wasn't so lucky. Looks like they shot him in the knees first to make him talk. Looks like a drug deal gone bad. When he wouldn't give it up, they shot her in the chest. It didn't look like they got what they came for, so they shot him in the chest," Hanky said. "That one most likely killed him, or he had a heart attack after seeing the woman shot."

"We heard four gunshots after we pulled up. We were hunkered down in my car," I said. I wondered out loud, "Where was the dog through all this? He couldn't have been in the house while the gunmen were."

"I think the dog was in the back yard when it started and opened the screen door to get at the intruders," Hanky said. "The outside of the screen door is pretty scratched up. When that dog came bounding inside, he might be what saved the woman from being shot again."

Detective Taylor walked up. Taylor and I had a history of me crashing his homicide cases much like people who crash weddings. Like wedding crashers, I was always uninvited and was always asked to leave—not that I ever did…leave, that is.

"Good evening, Ms. Alexander," Taylor said. "I should've guessed you'd be the one to find these two, especially after I heard there was a dog involved. The dog didn't shoot them, did he?"

"Funny. The dog was the one who got shot," I said.

"How did you know there was a dog shot?" Hanky

asked Taylor.

"Yeah, how did you?" I asked.

"A witness across the street saw you two getting what he said looked like a dead dog in your car," he said answering both of us.

"Well, then, this neighbor should be able to describe the two who came out of the house because one guy shot the dog while the other ran to his side of the street to get in the car behind the wheel," I said.

"Nope. Says he didn't see or hear anything," Taylor said.

Hanky made a harrumph sound. "Well, the Neighborhood Watch around here is watching in this neighborhood, just not talking to the police."

"Then how did he know we put a dog in my car?" I asked.

He opened his leather-bound notebook, unlike the dollar store ones Hanky used. Taylor made a giant effort to flip to the page in his notebook and recite the neighbor's statement. "He said, he walked outside for a 'breath of fresh air,' his words exactly, and that's when he saw two white women taking what looked like a dead dog off in a BMW." He looked up at me adding, "One of the white women he described would be you. He also gave me your license plate."

"He had to have heard all four gunshots like we did. Instead, he strolled out for what, fresh air, and just happened to remember THAT license plate?" I asked. I knew that neighbor was lying, but this was a job Ava was good for since she had an ability to tell when anyone was lying. She didn't make that public, but I had known it since we were kids. I made a mental note to go talk to this neighbor…tomorrow or the day after.

"I can't beat what he saw out of him," he said.

"What about the neighbor on the other side of the double? They had to hear something," I said.

"No one's home on the other side. We'll keep checking but if he's not home, he probably won't have much to offer," Hanky said.

I stood there listening to Detectives Taylor and Hanky talk about the crime scene while I looked around the front yard of the home where the shooting took place. There was a small, round, metal bistro table and chairs, nice but not expensive, sitting on the front porch. There was a chain through the legs of the chairs and the table locking them to a porch railing. In the small, well maintained garden on the front side of the double where the shootings took place, were flowers planted around a statue of the Virgin Mary, Mother of Jesus. The car in their driveway was an older Honda about eight to ten years old. It had a couple of small dinks, and scratches but otherwise no damage from accidents. It looked clean and well kept. There was a school decal on the rear window.

"Can I see inside their house?" I asked no one in particular.

"Why?" Hanky asked.

"Because something out here doesn't feel right, and

I want to see if I get the same vibe inside."

Hanky shrugged and made a face that suggested she didn't care if I went inside. She was looking around until she spotted the forensics' guy taking photos of the blood on the lawn.

Taylor said, "I'll take you inside."

"Ava's been in. I want to go look around. It will only take a minute." Hanky was about to say something, but I beat her to it, "And I won't touch anything," I said.

"Good," she said and walked off to speak to the tech.

Upon entering, there was a double room that was used for a living room and dining room that led to a hall with a bath off it. A bedroom was behind the hall bath. Another room was after the bedroom, either a second bedroom or sitting room, with a kitchen at the rear room of the house. There was a large dog bed, food and water bowls in the second bedroom with Volker's name on them. I walked through to the backyard. It was small, divided in half with a fence giving one small yard for each side. There was another big water bowl sitting at the bottom of the steps. There was a back exit with a screen door that was askew. It was not square to the opening, so it didn't close tightly. It had a lot of scratches and a smart dog could figure out how to get it to open in order to run inside. It looked like the kind of screen door on my parents' home…in need of repair. If you hit it hard enough, it would pop open enough for a dog to get his head in. It looked like Volker knew how to open it.

Aside from the blood all over an area rug where I assumed the shootings took place, the home was relatively neat. The bed was made and there were no dishes in the sink. The living room had a modest size sofa, a nice chair, both facing a flat screen TV, not very big. There were much bigger models out there. There was a low-end stereo system under what looked like a homemade TV stand.

"Did you find any drugs or paraphernalia?" I asked.

"No, but we're still looking," Taylor said.

"Any guns?" I asked.

"No. I know what you're thinking," Taylor said. "Humor me and let's hear it our loud."

"Look at this place. For one, it hasn't been tossed so the shooters wanted info, I'm guessing," I said.

"Maybe they weren't here long enough to look for drugs or the money," Taylor said.

"Secondly," I continued, "does it look like drug dealers live here? If they are, they must be the worse dealers on the planet. Don't most have at least a big screen TV, big, fancy, SUV with tricked out wheels, and a big, loud boom box for a stereo that could blow the hair off your head? This place has a nice, girly type bedspread and family pictures and a Crucifix over the mirror in the bedroom."

"Hmmm," was all Taylor contributed. He let me go on.

"The Honda outside is a conservative car with a Delgado College parking sticker on the back windshield. One of them goes to the community college. There's a religious shrine in the front yard of the Madonna. How many gangbanger/drug dealers do you know with a shrine and a small screen TV who go to college?" I asked.

"Something is off. Maybe they hit the wrong house," Taylor said tapping his Mont Blanc pen on the notepad.

"The wrong house is a possibility, or it could have been a hit. Maybe someone wanted these two gone," I said. "These people don't have much and what they have is well cared for. What about the woman's purse?" I asked nodding to the purse and contents all over the living room floor. "Do you know what their names are, or where they worked?"

"We haven't finished processing the scene," Taylor said as we both headed toward the area where the purse was on the floor.

Just looking, without touching any of the contents, we could see a name badge for the woman indicating she was a student/worker at Delgado.

"Good call," Taylor said. "They took the male victim out of here a few minutes before you came back. He was wearing a name badge indicating he worked as a manager at the chain grocery story on Carrollton Avenue, the one not far from here."

"Rouses?"

"Yeah, that's it," he said.

I shrugged my shoulders. "This just looks all wrong. Look around. These two don't look like they were into drugs," I said. "What about who lives on the other side of this common wall?"

"We're looking for him. He's not home, but we know who he is, and he's got a sheet," Taylor said. "You know, you could just let the police handle this."

"That's a great idea. I'll take it under advisement. You know, I bet, that neighbor who saw us take the dog saw a lot more than he's telling," I said.

Hanky came in. "Find anything?" she asked.

"It's what we're not finding here," Taylor said.

"Oh, I just spoke to Dante," she said. "He said after I get your statement to tell you to…"

"Stay out of it," we both said at the same time.

"Okay… seems his recent head injury didn't affect his memory," I said.

Chapter Four

Still Friday

UNIVERSITY MEDICAL CENTER is the big…emphasis on big…new medical facility that took the place of Charity after Katrina. It's a behemoth. While Charity was a twenty-story tall facility, it only took up one square block. University took up eight, city blocks of real estate with six-story, glass buildings. It felt like it spanned an eternity to walk from one end—where you needed to park—to the other end— where you had to go.

I met up with Jiff just inside the Emergency Department. We got to the ED within minutes of each other. We both looked hot and tired, like we'd walked across the Sahara Desert. Even though it was winter in New Orleans, we were having an unusually warm day, eighty degrees unusual. So, you wanted to wear winter clothes this time of year because when else can you wear them? So, we pull out the lightweight wools and sweaters even though we would be more comfortable in sundresses and shorts.

Walking across blocks in and out of the buildings

trying to find the department they took the girl and Ava to was daunting, and hot. Finally, I called Ava's cell and asked her where in that health care maze was she. She informed me she had no idea where she was as she didn't have a window to look out of when they arrived in the ambulance. She handed her cell to a nurse asking her to give me directions. The nurse advised how to get to the area of the Medical Center where *all gunshot victims are always brought.* She made that clear several times. I guess she thought if I had one friend brought in with a gunshot wound, I might have more in the future.

I was directed to the building at the opposite end of the vast medical center where I parked. This is like my luck at airports, when my gate is always the farthest one at the end whatever concourse my flight leaves from.

The Emergency Department was filled with people sitting in every chair, sitting on the floor, or leaning on the wall. My guess, it would get worse as the night progressed. This is where all gunshot cases were now being treated, so a big Friday night would generate more business as it wore on.

I did a fast look over the people sitting and standing and was about to look for a place to park myself when Taylor and Hanky spotted me. Taylor made a direct path in my direction while Hanky followed a little less enthusiastically. Over their shoulder, I could see Jiff as he stepped into the doorway and did the visual scan looking for me.

"Now, you're getting Ava involved in your crime hunts?" Taylor asked as he and Hanky walked up.

"Who's Ava?" asked Hanky.

"Crime scenes find me, I don't go looking, I swear!"

"I'm not inclined to believe that," Hanky said.

"You know, if I take the stairs in all public buildings, no telling what or who else I might find," I said.

"You didn't answer my question," Hanky said crossing her arms across her chest. "Ava?"

"Ava Frost is a new member of my team at work who is moving back to New Orleans from New York. I've known her since grade school. Dante remembers her too, for that matter," I said. "Didn't you see her at the crime scene? She stayed with the victim that went in the ambulance."

"I know who you mean. I saw her. I thought she was one of the victims or a neighbor. I didn't meet her," Hanky said. "You two Nosy Nellies should make a great team."

Little did Hanky know that Ava's ability to tell when someone was lying was going to work great with my ability to see what's incongruous in patterns or situations.

"I met her once when I worked in New York," Taylor said. "She did some fraud investigation at my brother's firm and we all went out for a drink after. She's all right."

"Isn't that grand?" asked Hanky. "Taylor gives this Ava his seal of approval, while Brandy takes her under her wing so they can find crime scenes together."

Taylor just shook his head and added, "She's a nice girl."

"Ask Dante," I said.

"I will," Hanky said. "Where is she so we can question her?"

"Ava is sitting right over there next to the vending machine," I said. "The nurse at the desk told me the victim only let go of her arm after they gave her a sedative," I said.

"I'll go talk to her and take her statement. She might remember me," Taylor said as he turned to head in her direction.

"Before you go, can you tell me what their names are—the two victims?" I asked.

Taylor and Hanky looked at each other, then Taylor said, "Nina and Carlos Perez. Carlos was pronounced dead at the scene. He was twenty-six. Nina Perez is nineteen. Not sure, yet, if they were married, partners, or brother and sister." Then, he walked off in Ava's direction.

"You know, they had a big dog for protection and a holy statue in the front yard for all the good it did them," Hanky said.

I moved to the more immediate question I wanted answered, and that was, did Taylor know about Ava's secret skill. I wanted to put her to work on a conversation with Hanky to get a better perspective. I'd find out later from Ava if Taylor tried lying to her. Taylor didn't strike me as that kinda guy. Lie to perps, yes. Lie to women in general, no. Then, I stopped to think, how would I know? I don't have that skill, Ava does.

WE WAITED IN the hospital emergency room area until a nurse came and told Ava, Nina had just calmed down due to the sedative and would likely be quiet all night. She suggested we come back in the morning. Ava and I left our contact numbers if there was any new information or if the lady awoke and asked for us.

"Hey, it's only 8:30, are you guys hungry?" Jiff asked. "I'll take you to dinner. We can go to Morton's in Canal Place or sit in the lobby at the Westin and get drinks and order appetizer small plates. We can drop Ava at Julia's Bed and Breakfast on our way home."

Ava looked at me and nodded.

"Sounds great to me," I said.

The three of us took off on what felt like a pilgrimage back to the cars. We came to Jiff's car first. Mine was still a good block away. We decided to go in his car, and he could drop us both back at mine on the way home.

I could give Ava a ride back to Julia's Bed and Breakfast, where I had made her a reservation on behalf of the company during the process of her transfer back to New Orleans until she found an apartment.

THE LOBBY CHAIRS in the Westin were so comfortable. Jiff dropped us and went to park. Ava and I sat looking out the ceiling to floor windows at the ships passing below on the Mississippi. The view of the turns in the river were amazing from the sixth-floor lobby of this hotel. By the time our drinks came, a glass of wine for Ava and me, Jiff walked up to join us.

"Before I drink this, because it might put me to sleep after a long week ending with this day, tell me what's going on with your wedding plans," Ava said.

"We had a date set, but the venue was taken over by termites, and we had to cancel that place," I said. "That was just a couple of months ago and trying to find a place over the holidays was next to impossible."

Jiff went to the restaurant at the other end of the hotel lobby and returned with a menu for each of us. We looked over them in silence while we decided what we wanted to eat. After a few minutes Ava said, "I really don't want a lot to eat."

I agreed, so we ordered a couple of appetizer plates to share. Jiff knew I didn't like to eat late, and Ava didn't look like she was a big eater from the size of her small frame. Jiff ordered himself a hamburger.

"So, here's to being back in New Orleans and to you helping me," she said as we clinked our glasses. "Now tell me why you haven't rescheduled your wedding."

"We found a house to move into, and it didn't pass inspection right about the time that the location for the wedding/reception—and it belongs to my family I might add—came under attack of some fierce, fast moving termites," Jiff said. "And that's the Reader's Digest version."

"Yeah. Finding a place in November, right before the holidays on short notice was daunting. The house we thought we were buying fell through. Every venue in town was booked for the holidays through February with Mardi Gras Krewes having reserved rooms for their balls and parties. We thought we'd wait until after Mardi Gras to see about setting a date. Then the pandemic hit mid-March, so here we are," I said. "It's hard to find anywhere that will let us have more than ten people in attendance. I really don't want to get married wearing a mask and have a reception via Zoom."

"My mother is a judge. She could marry us, and we could have a reception or just a party later, when everything goes back to normal," Jiff said.

"I'm thinking the same thing," I said. "I don't want a wedding and reception where we, you and I, in addition to all the guests need to wear masks while standing six feet apart!"

"Wow, you two have had a string of bad luck," Ava said.

"Yes. The score currently is World – 2. Brandy and Jiff – 0," I said.

"Just everyday stuff we need to deal with," Jiff said. "I want whatever Brandy wants for a wedding. It doesn't change our plan. Our plan is to get married and spend the rest of our lives together."

He leaned over and kissed me. He always knew the right thing to say.

"I wanted to ask you, Ava, if you haven't found a place yet, do you want to stay at my condo until you do or it sells, whichever comes first. You can stay there until it sells…which might take a few months in this pandemic since showings will likely be virtual."

"There is floor to ceiling windows with great views like here. Only the view is Lake Pontchartrain, not the Mississippi River," I said nodding to the windows with the tremendous view of the meandering great waterway.

"Why aren't you two living there?" she asked.

"We have two dogs, and the Penthouse is on the fourteenth floor. That makes walking dogs via the elevator tiresome. We're looking for a house with a yard," I said, "and a doggie door."

"Isabella and I moved in with Brandy and Meaux…" Jiff started to say.

"And Suzanne," I added. "You remember her, don't you? She lived in a big, white two-story house on the corner of our block."

"Oh, yeah. She always had some strange pets. I remember, her," she said. "And a lot of brothers."

"We all live together," Jiff continued "until we find and close on a house. The only downside to staying at the condo is you need to leave the place showable just in case we get an offer, and they want a walk thru before they write it."

"I'm pretty neat," Ava said. "I always make my bed

after I get up and I hate dishes in the sink. That shouldn't be a problem. This would really help me, even if it's just a couple of weeks. I can take a bit more time to find a place to rent."

"Great," Jiff said. "We'll come get you tomorrow and take you to see it."

"That would be great," she said. "If you pick me up early enough, I'll treat you two to coffee and croissants at Croissant d'Or."

"You can take the streetcar to meet me there or I can stop and pick you up," I said.

"I must admit, I've taken the streetcar there every morning this week for my daily fix of coffee with chicory and a big, warm, buttery croissant before I walk over to the office," Ava said with a big smile. "I could only get coffee with chicory at one grocery in all of New York. It was expensive, but it was my guilty pleasure."

"Doesn't Frank make coffee and breakfast every morning at the Bed and Breakfast?" I asked.

"Yes, but I get up early and get out of there before the screaming starts. I like the short streetcar ride, and once I get a car, I probably won't be taking it that much," she said. "I'd like to take it again, tomorrow morning."

"We'll meet up with you at 9:00 a.m." I said. "I wondered how long it would take you to migrate to your favorite French bakery."

"We'll see you there," Jiff said as he dropped Ava

and I off at my car back at the hospital where I parked.

Jiff said goodnight to Ava as she got in on the passenger side of my car. Jiff kissed me saying in my ear, "I'll see you at home. Does that poor girl know what you've gotten her into?"

Chapter Five

Saturday morning

I GOT A call at 6:30 a.m. the next morning long before my alarm was set to go off. It was Ava on the other end telling me an ED nurse named Lillie Ray called her cell asking if she could come back to the hospital. Nina Perez woke up screaming for her.

"I'm on my way. I'll pick you up and go with you," I said. "Croissants will have to wait."

Jiff jumped up and started to dress when I answered the phone. "I'll take you. It will be faster to get in and see Nina if you don't have to park," he said. He drove me to pick Ava up at Julia's bed and breakfast and dropped us off near the entrance to the medical center building Nina Perez was in.

"Just call me when you're ready to leave. If I can't pick you up, I'll send the firm's driver," he said. Then, he went home to take care of our furry kids. I stayed with Ava at the hospital. We hadn't had a second alone or away from anyone for me to ask her what she found out about the woman, if anything. The one thing I knew Ava would discover is whether the young woman was lying.

I also thought if the girl was that traumatized, it might help her to tell someone, not as imposing as the police, what happened. It would also help us figure out what she knew and what she didn't know about the people who attacked the two of them. I wanted to help her and her dog.

My motives to tag along with Ava were largely selfish as I knew Ava could tell right away if this young woman knew her attackers or had any sort of dealings with them, good or bad.

JIFF DROPPED US and we spent the morning at the hospital. By the time we got there, Nina Perez had been given a sedative again only to wake up sporadically in a medicated fog asking where her husband was.

"If they were going to sedate her so heavily, why did they call you?" I wondered out loud. I didn't expect an answer.

Just then a nurse came in to check Nina's vitals and Ava asked her my question.

"It was a mild dose to calm her down. She should wake up in about ten to fifteen minutes or so. It's good you're here this time. She might remain calm when she sees you. She got hysterical when she was told her husband was dead," Nurse Lilly Ray said.

"Did the police talk to her yet?" I asked.

"Not that I'm aware. I was here all night. They left a number to call when she wakes up. I'll give them a call before I leave and let them know she should be awake. Someone else will look in on her," Nurse Lillie Ray said.

When she turned to go, I asked if she could wait to call the number for the police, if possible. I added, she might be less afraid to tell us what she remembers. Lillie Ray smiled at me and left.

"Ava, I hope you have a calming effect on this gal when she wakes up so we can get a few answers," I said. "I'm also hoping we can talk to her before the police get here and put the kibosh on us seeing her."

"What did you hear about the dog? Anything?" she asked.

"Nothing yet," I said as I checked my watch before I picked up my cell to dial the vet. "We've been moving at light speed since yesterday. The time totally flew by me until you just said it. There's usually someone there by 7:30 a.m. I hope one of the vets or a tech can give me an update."

After a brief hold, Kelly told me Dr. Kevin was checking on Volker now. Dr. Kevin came on the call and said he was still in critical condition, but he was hopefully optimistic because the dog was so strong.

"Well, the good news is he made it through the night. Kelly said they would know more and call with an update after lunch," I said.

"That's something positive to tell this woman when we talk to her since the news about Carlos was not good." she asked.

"I saw a photo of the two of them on her dresser," I told her. "He had his arm around her like they were a happy couple."

"Yeah, I only got as far as the front room where they were shot," Ava said.

"Hey, I wanted to ask you what did you think of Detective Taylor? He said he knew you from New York?"

"Oh yeah. Small world, huh? I did some work for his brother's firm when I was an analyst with the FBI. His bro is a big-time investment guy…worth billions if I had to guess," Ava said. "He's as good looking as your detective friend and they both wore nice, I mean, really nice, clothes," she added shaking her hand to suggest he was hot stuff. "The brother would send his driver in the company car to pick me up and bring me wherever I had to go after our appointments… the company car was a Rolls."

"You should have set your sights on the investment brother. You wanted to leave all that to come back here…because…?" I asked.

"I missed the humidity."

"And the brutally hot summers?" I asked.

"Yes, I almost forgot those," she said laughing. "I came back to take care of my dad and be here for him. Besides, of the two brothers, the one here is nicer."

"Oh, so you followed the nice one back here. He is nice, but he has Yankee manners."

"What? Yankee manners?"

"Yeah, or lack thereof. It's not that he's rude. He just doesn't always do what we've come to expect here, like opening your car door. I'm just spoiled living here in New Orleans. Wait until you see how he measures up to some of these local boys whose mothers raised them right," I said laughing.

"I think Travis's manners are just fine," she said.

"Well, the brother must manage Taylor's investments since His Gucci-ness could never afford the way he dresses, or that high end Mercedes he drives, on a NOPD salary," I said. "Is he honest? I know you can tell."

"Based on the dealings I've had with him; he's been a standup guy. I haven't dated him and that's usually where the wheels come off for me," she said laughing. "Why? Are you interested in dating him?"

"Oh God, no! I have had lots of dealings with him and Hanky and they've all felt good…honest…like he's been straight with me. I just wanted the inside scoop," I said laughing. "If the brother comes to visit Taylor here in New Orleans maybe we can set him up with Julia."

"I like his brother," Ava said. "What did he ever do to you?"

"That means you have a good, fast read on Julia. Okay, maybe we set him up with Hanky. She looks good when she fixes herself up," I said.

"Detective Taylor's partner? The woman cop? I haven't talked to her at all, but I'll let you know when I do," she said.

Nurse Lillie Ray, who was about to leave, came over to us and said, "You can go in to see her now. She's waking up."

Nina Perez was a petit woman, attractive with long dark hair. She was sitting up when we walked in, awake. She had been shot in the shoulder. She looked a bit confused when she saw us wearing masks, but she immediately recognized Ava from her red hair.

"Remember me?" Ava said. "How are you feeling?"

"Thank you, for helping me," Nina said. "A nurse told me Carlos didn't make it. Those men shot him three times."

"They shot you, too. Do you remember?" I said nodding to her.

"Yes…I do remember. I remember the dog chased them out of there," she said tearing up. "Where's the dog? Did they kill him?"

"I took Volker to my vet on Magazine Street," I said. "They are taking very good care of him. He's the only witness besides you."

"Oh, my God! The dog! I remember him running past me," she said. "They shot him too?"

"Yes, but so far, he's hanging in there. One of those men shot him in the chest out on your front lawn. We saw it."

"Poor dog. They should just put him out of his misery," she said, then asked, "What about Carlos?" She dabbed at her eyes with a tissue.

I was taken aback by someone wanting to put their

dog down when there was a chance, he would make it, especially after a trauma like this. The one left wanted to keep as much of what they had together, especially a pet. It seemed no one told her about her husband, but she knew.

Ava just shook her head and quietly said, "When I found you, Carlos wasn't breathing. I called an ambulance but there was nothing they could do for him."

Nina cried but the medication must have still had her sedated because she was not as hysterical as I expected her to be.

"Can you tell us what happened?" Ava asked her after several minutes while holding her hand.

Nina wiped her eyes again and cleared her throat. "Carlos and I just got home. I picked him up from the store after I left my job at Delgado, around 5:15. He gets off at 5:30 from the grocery store. It works out perfectly with only one car. I take classes there in the morning and work afternoons in the library to pay for my tuition."

We let her tell us at her own speed.

"We walked inside, and I had just gone to the kitchen to let the dog out into the backyard. I heard voices, so I came back to the living room and two men were inside waving guns at Carlos. They had on hoodies and one of those stretchy caps, a ski mask I think it's called, that was pulled down to hide their faces," she said. "They kept saying they wanted to know where something was. They kept saying, 'we know she gave it to you.' I thought we were being robbed, but then one said, 'we will make you tell us.'"

"What were they talking about? Could you tell?" I asked.

"At first I thought they were talking about money, but they never took Carlos's wallet or asked for my purse," she said. She started crying again.

"Take your time," Ava said pouring a glass of water and holding it so Nina could take a sip from the straw offered to her.

"I thought they wanted money for drugs, but the way they were talking, and shooting Carlos in the legs, they wanted him to tell them something. It sounded like they thought Carlos knew where something was or took something. Carlos and I never use drugs. He didn't know what they wanted, or what they were talking about," she said starting to sniffle again.

"I know," I said standing on the other side of the hospital bed. Nina grabbed my hand. She had my hand in her left one and Ava's in her right one. All I wanted was to make this right for this poor girl and bring back her Carlos. It was something I would never be able to do.

"Did you recognize these guys from your neighborhood, or do you think you or Carlos knew them?" Ava asked.

"I couldn't tell who they were with the ski masks on, and I don't think Carlos knew who they were either. He kept saying, 'I don't know who you are or what you're talking about'," Nina said.

"How long have you lived at that double?" I asked.

"We moved there not long ago. After we signed a year lease and moved in, we realized the neighborhood was not what we expected. We noticed a lot of drugs and the kind of people we try to avoid. But we signed a lease for a year, so we couldn't move unless we bought out our lease and we didn't have the money to do that."

"How did your dog get back inside the house? You said you went to the kitchen to let him out" I asked.

"Carlos always said Volker knows if he hits the screen door with his paws, it will pop open wide enough for him to get his head through. He usually just lets himself back inside. He's really Carlos's dog. He's been doing that since he was a puppy…opening our screen doors. I think he did it when he heard me scream after they shot Carlos."

"I'm so sorry," Ava said.

"If Volker hadn't come running and barking, I think they would have shot me again. One was aiming for me when he heard the back-door slam" she said. "That's the last thing I remember until I heard you come in to help us."

"Do you remember anything about the two men, like tattoos on their hands or any part of their body you could see?" I asked.

"No, I didn't see any tattoos," she answered. "They wore gloves and masks."

"You mentioned they wore masks. Could you tell if they were white, black, Latino or Asian?" I asked.

"I only looked at the guns pointing at us. I didn't see their skin. I'm sorry, I don't remember," she said.

"What about a smell, or something on their clothes, hat, shoes? Work shoes, logos on shirt or hats?" I asked her.

"I don't remember any smell or logo or tattoo or anything other than the very big guns they shot us with. They were big and loud. I only looked at the guns," she said again and started crying.

"Accents?" I asked. "Could you tell if they were white, black or Hispanic?"

Nina shook her head no. Ava nodded toward the door, and we decided to let her rest. The police were going to be there soon and ask her the same stuff all over again.

"Hey, we're going to go and let you rest, but one more question. Do you know your neighbor's name who lives on the other side of your double?" I asked her.

"No, he's never home much, but when he is, it's late and he has his stereo on loud. Carlos met him when he went to ask him to lower it because we must get up early. Carlos said he was rude about it. He barely turned it down after he asked," Nina said and started to dab at her eyes with a tissue again.

"Will you be okay if we leave you now?" Ava asked.

"I think so," Nina said nodding and dabbing her

eyes.

"If it's OK, I'll leave you both of our cell numbers in case you think of anything else," I said.

"Thank you," Nina said. "Thank you for taking care of the dog, but really, he should be put out of his misery."

"You're talking to a rescuer for your breed of dog," Ava said. "She'll tell you if Volker's quality of life plummets."

I pulled out a business card and wrote my personal cell and Ava's on the back. "The police will be here soon to ask you what you remember, but call me or Ava anytime you need to talk, okay?"

At the elevator, I asked Ava, "Did you notice she always referred to Volker as the dog, and never by name?"

"Well, she said it was Carlos's dog, so maybe she didn't have an attachment."

"Yeah, well, she was in a hurry to put him down, or 'out of his misery'. Strange thing to say about the dog that she just finished saying saved her life."

The elevator doors opened and there was Hanky and Taylor stepping off on their way to see Nina Perez.

"What are you two still doing here?" Hanky asked.

"We actually went home and came back," I said.

"The nurse called at 5:30 a.m. saying Nina was hysterical and asking for me. I called Brandy for a ride. She seems to be doing better now," Ava said giving a big angelic smile.

Chapter Six

Saturday

AVA'S FIRST WEEK back in New Orleans involved her setting up her banking, filling out a ton of company paperwork with Personnel, checking into Julia's Bed and Breakfast on the reservation I made for her, getting a comprehensive tour of the new Medical Facility, happened upon a shooting, riding in an ambulance with a gunshot victim, and getting on a first name basis with the police who came to investigate the shooting. I thought she was off to a good start. She would be up to speed with me in no time when it came to crime scenes.

Jiff had said to me he felt bad for Ava and didn't want her to turn and run back to New York. He didn't know she was committed to staying here for her dad, otherwise, I would have bet money on Julia and Frank sending her screaming back to the Big Apple. I needed Ava here, so I had to find her a place to live, fast.

Knowing how thoughtful Jiff can be, I'm sure offering his condo to Ava was his way of trying to save her from overexposure to Frank and Julia. His condo was the Penthouse apartment overlooking Lake Pontchartrain and had been featured in New Orleans Magazine. It was the perfect short-term solution.

Ava and I left Nina and the Medical Center close to eleven, just in time for an early lunch since we hadn't had breakfast.

"You know we could go to Croissant d'Or now. They serve a great lunch, in addition to breakfast," I said.

"Deal, and it's my treat. Jiff bought me dinner last night."

We grabbed a taxi. It didn't take us long before we were sitting at a table in the very French and stylish patisserie on Ursulines Avenue in the French Quarter known as Croissant d'Or. I was having their traditional Quiche Lorraine and Ava ordered a croissant with turkey. This French bakery had remained the same over the years and that was a good thing. To me, their claim to fame was their croissants and apple strudel they made for the Deutsches Haus. They made a killer strudel I always bought at Oktoberfest. I brought some home with me every year.

"You know I'm very grateful you helped me get back here with a job," Ava said between bites. "A good job."

"I'm not sure you will still feel grateful after a few more weeks here. Between staying at Julia's B&B, our big adventure yesterday with your apartment search, the pandemic—having to wear masks and it is making it harder to work—are you sure you want to stay in New Orleans?" I asked. "You're lucky you moved here in what is our winter. The summers are intolerable."

"Well, March in New York, I wouldn't just be wearing only a long sleeve blouse like I am now to go outdoors," she said. "The virus is worse in New York than here."

"Yes, but it's a matter of statistics. More people in NYC mean more who test positive with it," I said. "We're getting our fair share of positive results here because we're so social, I think."

"While it might look like I jumped into the fire, remember the frying pan for me is New York City. With people stacked on top of each other, it's impossible to stay six feet apart from anyone. You can't walk down the street without people bumping into you constantly. The elevator in my building was so small, if two people were in it at the same time, we were pressed against each other. I never met my neighbors because I always waited for the next elevator even before the pandemic!"

"I guess you could have taken the stairs," I said.

"Stairwells are narrow so you can't get far away from anyone, even if far away is only six feet. You pass almost shoulder to shoulder in stairwells. Not to mention, I lived on the twelfth floor. That's a lotta stairs. Going down wasn't a problem unless you were carrying stuff. Most of the friends I made in college all moved away. Even if they are in New Jersey or

Connecticut, it's hard to see them unless you plan out a weekend visit. There's no hooking up after work for a glass of wine or a beer. That's called G.U… geographically undesirable. Here, at least, I have long time friends with you and Suzanne. I feel like I've left off where we were, friendship wise, when I moved. I have two new friends in Frank and Julia, and who knows what will develop with Detective Taylor. There was a spark there when I first met him, but then he moved here. I also have my dad here," she said as we lifted our glasses and clinked a toast.

"You're right. Even though New Orleanians will move back if we get transferred elsewhere, a lot of our old friends from high school and grade school are hard to find now, after Katrina. Many left Orleans Parish and went to Metairie, and believe it nor not, the Northshore," I said.

"The Northshore?"

"That's the other side of Lake Pontchartrain, across the twenty-four-mile bridge. It's now a bedroom community to New Orleans. And, you know what, they still work on this side."

"They live on the Northshore and work over here? Really?" Ava asked.

"Yep. I bet you never thought you could get there from here, right?"

"Wow, people travel that bridge back and forth every day to work on this side?" she asked.

I nodded.

"Well, I guess it's about the same commute as those in New Jersey who take the train into Manhattan to work." she said. "Only on trains you can work, sleep or read. I guess you can't do that on the bridge."

"It takes a while, but you'll start to run into some of your old pals," I said. "More and more businesses are moving over there or opening an office. This is New Orleans, after all. Just listen for the yat-speak."

"True dat," Ava said between bites of her turkey croissant.

"Spoken like a real yat, dahlin'," I said. "I guess it's like riding a bike. You never forget it."

A few months ago, right before the pandemic started, Ava told me in an email she wanted to move back to New Orleans as her dad had had a stroke and she had no one here to look after him or visit him in the nursing home. She asked me to help her find a job she could transfer to within the company. I did. As soon as her hardship transfer papers were signed, she had a post here. I don't think the ink was dry on her paperwork when the door slammed shut on all company relocations due to the pandemic. She was lucky.

After high school, Ava got a scholarship to NYU and I went to Loyola of the South. After college she went to work in New York as an analyst for the FBI. She was sent to all kinds of training for reading people, listening to voice inflections, everything to help with interrogating criminals.

She hated it. After a couple of years, she managed

to get a job for the same big telecom company in New York that I worked for in New Orleans. We'd see each other at least once a year at the big sales conference held in some big city. Ava and I would use this trip and extend our stay a couple of days to catch up with each other. These trips helped us to maintain our lifelong friendship with yearly face to face contact along with emails, birthday and Christmas cards.

Ava was hard to miss in first grade mainly because she didn't participate or play with anyone, and she had fiery red hair. Kids teased her about her hair, so she watched. The first week of school, she sat by herself in the cafeteria, stood alone on the playground and walked to and from school alone. She had no siblings. No one liked her after they played with her because she'd call them out when they lied to her—even if it was a small lie often told on playgrounds. She could always tell when someone was lying.

We became friends the day I sat next to her in the cafeteria and offered her half of the candy bar my dad always put in my lunch box. We stayed friends because I never lied to her, not even to protect her feelings.

"We should make a formidable team working on the same accounts finding fraudulent activity," I said. "With my ability to see irregularities in calling patterns or situations and you knowing when a client might be hiding the truth…"

"I notice you didn't say lying," she interjected. "Over the years, I've become quite jaded after hearing all the lies people will tell, men in particular. The real sad part about lying is that most often they don't even need to. It's just part of their nature. It has become part of my nature to avoid them."

"Correct. If a client is hiding the truth, or his employees are, we should be able to make short work of several new cases that just logged into our department," I said.

"It will be great working together," she said.

"Yes, and I need help now if I'm ever going to plan...correction...re-plan my wedding. I'm so ready to just let Jiff's mother marry us."

"Weddings can be tricky when it comes to families," Ava said.

"Then you do remember my mother," I said. "She has not gotten any better."

"I thought she'd be thrilled you are getting married."

"Well, she might be if she knew or if I was marrying Dante, and, if my sister hadn't already gotten married while producing grandkids. The grandchild has her as happy as she could ever be. She tried to talk me into making Dante marry me at a double wedding with my sister and his brother. Dante's brother, who had to marry my sister I might add. Her reason was she didn't want to pay for a second wedding...mine."

"OMG!"

"Yep, and my dad almost fainted. I really don't know what he ever saw in my mother to marry her and then stay married to her. He has the patience of Job."

Just then my phone rang. I said, "It's the vet. I gotta take this."

Ava called over a waiter and paid our check while I got an update on Volker.

When I hung up, I said, "Do you want me to drop you at the Westin or do you want to come with me to the vet. He says he's got some blood and tissue DNA he collected from Volker. Maybe the police can use it."

"I'm with you. I'd like to see this thing through."

"Great. Afterwards, we can go take a look at Jiff's apartment and you can see if you want to move into it."

"I'll want to move into it. Don't fret over that... I mean don't fret over dat, dahlin'," Ava said.

"You will fit right in. There are a few yats in Jiff's building and a lot in the building where we work. You'll fit right in!"

I CALLED DETECTIVE Taylor on our way to the vet's office and told him where we were going and asked if he could meet us. "The vet collected blood from the dog and some tissue from his teeth. I don't want to be the one to mess with the chain of evidence," I said.

"You will make a detective yet, Miss Alexander," he said. "I'm happy to swing by there and save you a trip."

"Well, Ava and I were headed there to see how Volker is doing, and I'll need to pay his bill. I also need to figure out when or where I can put him if he can come home."

"Oh, Ava's with you?" he asked without even trying to hide his enthusiasm about the chance of seeing her.

"Yes, she's with me," I answered giving Ava a wide-eyed—I-think-you-have-an admirer-look.

"Well, then, I'll head straight there," he said. "I'd like to see how the dog is doing too."

Who was he kidding? He liked Hanky's Schnauzer and my dog well enough. He was good around dogs, but I didn't see him going out of his way to visit a person in the hospital after he interrogated them, let alone a dog in a veterinary clinic.

This was all about Ava.

"Okay, then. See you at the vet clinic in about twenty minutes," I said and hung up. To Ava I said, "Someone has an admirer."

"You think Detective Taylor likes me?" she asked in her incredible to believe this fact tone.

"No, not you. Volker," I said smiling. "Maybe I can talk him into adopting him."

Chapter Seven

Saturday afternoon

WE CALLED FROM the vet's parking lot—the new procedure during pandemic times for appointments—Kelly answered and said we could come in. She brought us into an exam room right away and said Dr. Kevin or Dr. Scott would be right in. I advised her that a Detective Taylor would be meeting us. She said she would show him to this room when he arrived.

A few minutes later Taylor and an officer from Orleans Parish Animal Control followed Kelly into our exam room. They were followed by Dr. Scott and Dr. Kevin helping Volker walk a little with a sling. I recognized the Animal Control Officer as Casey Knox from my rescue work. We nodded at each other.

I made introductions all around. Dr. Scott left to help another patient. Taylor nodded at me, but he smiled at Ava.

"Hey Brandy," Dr. Kevin said. "We're being cautious with him using the sling. We don't want him opening any stitches since he's a big, young dog who is active and strong. He wants to move around, a lot."

"He looks great," I said.

Ava nodded in agreement. She went over to pet and rub Volker's head. "How long will he have to stay here?" I asked.

"He can stay as long as you need him to, but he could go home with you tomorrow or Monday. Is he staying with you?"

"I think he might have to. The owners were both shot along with Volker. The husband died at the scene, but his wife is at University Medical. I don't know when she will be released. She's a tiny woman who has a gunshot wound she will be recovering from."

Casey Knox said looking at Taylor, "If NOPD doesn't have a problem with your rescue fostering him, we won't either. We are slammed at the shelter and a big dog like this needs a lot of exercise and attention. I'll sign off to release Volker to Brandy."

"Thanks, Casey. I will need to find someone who can foster him," I said.

Dr. Kevin looked at me and nodded to Ava, "He weighs one-hundred-thirty pounds. It might take the two of you to handle him. He's strong."

"Yes. It took the two of us to get him in my car. He was dead weight so that was a struggle. Nina, the woman who was shot, weighs about ninety pounds, if that. She's a tiny gal."

"The good news is he's agreeable, and not mean. When he woke up, he just wagged that small tail of his and licked everyone's hand who came near him," he

said.

"Uh, that's not the dog we saw in action who got himself shot," I said. "He went after the gunman and grabbed his arm like he had been trained in combat. That reminds me, did you get anything, DNA, flesh, tissue, blood, anything from his teeth or around his mouth. I thought he might have some gunshot residue on his muzzle."

"I'm sure he did. I cut his beard where I saw blood and bagged it. There are also some swabs we took from inside his mouth. Besides blood and tissue, I think there was some fabric from a coat sleeve or shirt I found in his teeth," Dr. Kevin said. "I took what I found and placed each sample in an individual bag and marked it. I'll go get them for you."

Ava and I sat there petting and talking nice to Volker who did wag his tail for us and smiled a big toothy smile while panting from the exertion this short walk must have been for him. He was stoic and wouldn't let on he was in pain.

"He's a big dog," Taylor said.

"His imposing size could make anyone stop in their tracks before reaching out to pet him," Casey said.

"Yes, but he has a soft, gooey inside. He's only mean when he needs to be, and we've seen that side of him." I said.

Dr. Kevin brought back eight plastic bags with what he collected marked on each of them. He also had a sheet of paper for Taylor to sign saying he was in receipt of samples.

"I hope this will help the police catch whoever did this to him and his owners," I said. "Thank you."

"Actually, the department might want him to stay here until forensics looks at what you collected from him. They might want to come and do their own DNA test," Taylor said.

"Canine DNA is being used more and more to solve crimes. I'm sure they will want to verify Volker's DNA. The good news is that the possibility of another canine having the same DNA as this dog is less than one in a billion," Dr. Kevin said.

"Wow, I didn't realize that canine DNA could pinpoint an animal that close," I said.

"Right now, he's our best witness, our only witness who can ID the shooters," Taylor said. "Let me talk to the Captain and see if he'll spring for boarding this dog here or if he'll release him to you to foster. We might have to keep him at the precinct in the kennel," Taylor said.

"Oh no. He'll get depressed, and no one will walk or rehab him. This breed is very social, and they like interaction with humans. You just can't park him somewhere," I said, "like the police canine kennels."

"Brandy's right," Dr. Kevin said.

"I've come to realize she usually is," Taylor said.

"If you can't convince Dante to release him to me or pay to board him here, I repeat, here, not at the SPCA, or the police kennels, then I'll talk to him," I

said.

"Maybe the Captain will release him to me. I have a big yard," Taylor said.

"It takes more than a yard to foster a dog, especially a Giant Schnauzer. Even with rehabbing, he will still want and need a lot of exercise. Volker needs more attention and time to work on his recovery," I said.

"I can take care of him. I might need someone to brief me on what food to get, how often to walk him and stuff like that," he said and looked at Ava. "Other than work, I have time."

"Ava could help you!" I said a little too enthusiastically, not that Taylor noticed. "Ava has some time on her hands tomorrow before she starts her new job on Monday. Maybe she can help you get ready to foster him. This is only temporary until the owner says whether or not she will take him back."

"Yeah, sure, I'm happy to help you," Ava said shooting me a quick look out of the corner of her eye look. "I can even go over to your place and walk him on days you think you'll get home late."

I advised Dr. Kevin that I might need to leave Volker a few days until we work out the specifics, and he was fine with it.

Taylor mentioned, "Doctor, one of my techs might want to come and take a blood sample from this dog to make sure they are the same as what you're giving me." He added, when he saw the look of disbelief on my face, "Just standard police procedure."

"Sure thing," Dr. Kevin said. "Just tell them to ask for me, and I'll help them if they need it."

We thanked Dr. Kevin and on our way to the cars, Taylor said, "Oh, Ava. Here is my card, and why don't you give me your number to reach you later. I'm sure I'll have questions on food, you know, dog beds, other stuff he might need…"

"Water. Don't forget you have to give them fresh water every day," I said. "In a bowl. You need to place the bowl on the floor."

Neither commented but Ava had a smile leaking from the corner of her mouth.

Chapter Eight

Saturday Afternoon

I DROVE AVA to Jiff's condo in the high-rise overlooking Lake Pontchartrain. "I texted him and said we were on our way," I said to Ava. "He texted back saying he had already asked Sam to let us in if we got there first. He has to be the most thoughtful man I've ever met."

"Who's Sam?" Ava asked.

"He's Head of Security at the Towers. I knew Sam before I met Jiff. Sam adopted a mini-Schnauzer from me and named him Einstein because he thought the dog was so smart. I didn't know, but Jiff saw me talking with Sam and Einstein. He told me he was trying to figure out a way to get Sam to introduce us when he spotted me at a Mardi Gras parade," I said. "It was kismet."

"Yeah, that was some first meeting," Ava said shaking her head. "I remember you telling me how you met. It's sort of like what happened when you took me to look at that apartment yesterday. Do all of your outings turn into an adventure of a lifetime?"

"No," I said. "Not all. Wait until you see the view from his condo. You might even find an apartment in this building you want to rent or buy," I told her.

"Well, I really wanted to get a place close to where my dad is living so I won't always be driving to work or to see him. I could spend more time with him and have less stress," Ava said. "I'm going to visit him this evening and have dinner with him."

"That will be nice," I said, feeling bad for not remembering the whole reason Ava was moving back in the first place. "Your dad's staying at a place that is halfway between work and Jiff's condo. It will be on your way while you stay there."

Sam met us in the lobby and after a few exchanges to catch up and see how Einstein was doing, he took us up the elevator to Jiff's penthouse apartment.

"You didn't tell me it was da' penthouse," Ava said putting an accent on her y'at speak after we said goodbye to Sam, and he took the elevator back to his post in the lobby.

"Jiff and his family do everything, or go everywhere, first-class. If we had met on the Titanic, he would have been wearing a tuxedo to dinner, and I would have been with the Irish in steerage."

"You and me, both!" she said laughing.

I showed her around the apartment that took up the entire top floor of the building. There were four bedrooms, four baths, an office plus a dining room, and a large living room that opened into the kitchen with views of the lake from every angle.

"You have three outdoor, parking places assigned to this unit. They are covered but not enclosed. There's no inside parking, but there is a covered walkway to and from that area."

"I guess I can adapt," she sighed as if it was a major ordeal.

"Funny girl. Glass of wine while we wait?" I asked.

"Sure. White if you have it," Ava said. "Silly me, there's probably a wine cellar you haven't shown me."

"Actually, there is. It's a walk-in wine cooler in the kitchen. It looks like a cabinet or pantry. Come see."

After I showed her the wine cooler, we selected a chilled Spanish white wine that I found light and refreshing. We took our glasses to two big leather chairs facing each other in the living room with great views of the lake.

"So, why can't you reschedule in the place Jiff's family owns?" Ava asked.

"The ever so short version is this, the building is in the French Quarter which means it's under the purview of the French Quarter Commission. All repairs or improvements must be filed with the City of New Orleans and the Commission must approve them. That takes months by itself. First, they had to tent the building, about a square block, and then wait on approval for the repairs. With the pandemic and everything moving in slow motion at City Hall, it will be a miracle if it is back in commerce by next year," I

said.

"Tented, as in a circus tent?" she asked.

"Or bigger. I tried not to get involved in that process," I said.

"Thank goodness you didn't send out the invitations when that happened…or did you?"

"I was about to mail stamped and addressed invitations to 400+ people when the manager called me saying we had to reschedule, and it might be months before the building could be ready. I threw them in the trash right then and there."

"Oh, I'm sorry," Ava said.

"Dante found me a place that a friend was willing to let us have before he was injured at a crime scene."

"Dante?"

"Yes. You remember Dante? We dated, well sort of, in high school, and up until I met Jiff. We had worked through a lot and were finally on friendly ground when he was hit by a car fleeing a crime scene. That's another long story. I was involved in that case because of the body we found one night with an alligator hanging onto it."

"I've led such a plain vanilla life by comparison," Ava said smiling.

"Not really, you've worked for the FBI. Dante had a head injury that put him in a medically induced coma for weeks. I couldn't ignore his very generous gesture and Jiff and I decided to wait until he came out of the coma so he could tell me, himself, he got a place for us.

He only came out of the coma about a week before you got here."

"Wow, that's the short version? The unabridged version must be longer than a CVS receipt," Ava said laughing.

I looked at my wine glass. "I feel like guzzling this now that I'm talking about it. Jiff and I have pressed on trying to get past it all and now with the pandemic, it feels like it never ends."

"No, don't get past it. Get on with it. Isn't that what we used to say in high school when our team looked like we were about to lose? Then, we came back stronger. Let's figure it out," Ava said. "Decide what do you want to happen and then let's make it happen. I will help you."

"I have missed you," I said.

"You're gonna make me cry," Ava said.

"Before we plan the wedding, and I need your help on it to keep me focused, I want to ask you about Nina and Taylor. Did you pick up any hint from either of them not telling the truth?"

Ava took a sip of wine, put down her glass on the end table nearest her and scrunched up her face while looking at the ceiling. Finally, she said, "Nina is a puzzle. I have never had to deal with someone who has been shot before, so I'm not too sure if what I'm picking up are missing memory pieces, half-truths or what she thinks or wants to remember. I think she knows something she's not telling us, but did she lie? It feels like she's telling ninety percent of the truth with some lies in there, but I'm not sure it's intentional. She did seem confused at times with some of the memories of the event. Who wouldn't be? The drugs to sedate her aren't helping."

"People who have been shot sometimes take a while to remember the entire ordeal," I said. "She remembered the dog running through but not that Carlos was dead."

"That could be it," Ava answered. "You have more experience dealing with this sort of thing than I do."

"And what about Detective Taylor?" I asked taking a sip of wine. "Is he truthful?"

"Well, he has been so far. He's nice. Seems genuine. He appears the same as when we met in New York when I did some troubleshooting at his brother's firm. That was about a year ago. He was with some forensic team that was doing financial audits on accounting at his brother's firm. I think Taylor has an interest in the firm. It would explain what he can afford really nice things. Anyway, I was brought in to check out the network to see if it had been compromised. Taylor's brother is a bit of a character with the gig salesman personality. Likable. I didn't believe a lot of what his brother said, but he wasn't mean spirited, and I didn't think he outright lied. He's an exaggerator so there's always a hint of truth to what he's saying."

"The nice thing about Detective Taylor is his willingness to appreciate me bringing value or a different point of view to what's happened at a crime scene. Dante never wants me there. Hanky hates me interfering. We had a rough introduction when she first became Dante's partner that could have gone better," I said. "Our relationship has improved…well, from the way it started, the only option was up." We shared a laugh over that.

"Yeah, Hanky is going to be a harder read. She is wary, and watches what she says," Ava said picking up her glass again. "I know you don't want to ask, but I'm going to tell you because I think you want to know. Stop me if I'm wrong. What I remember about Dante from when we were in high school, is he is he leaves out information you would like or need to know to make a decent decision on your own. I remember him doing that to you in high school when you dated him. I'd have to see if he still does it."

"I'll save you the time. He still does it," I said taking a sip.

"I call that lying by omission. Many dispute that is lying, but to me, it still is."

"I agree, and I knew that about him after all these years. It's one of the main things that drove me crazy with him," I said. "That, and he hangs up without ever saying goodbye. You only know the call has ended when you hear dial tone."

"And Jiff? Do you want to know?" she asked very serious.

I nodded because I was afraid my voice would crack

when I said "No."

"He's a prince. He is so in love with you and honest in everything he says and does. Find me one like him, please," Ava said and reached for her glass.

"That was mean to make me think something else," I said balling up my cocktail napkin and throwing it at her.

"That's the thing about the truth. People think they want to know it, but when they find out what they didn't want to hear, they must either accept the lies or do something about it. That's why so many are happy living with not knowing," Ava said.

"As much as it would hurt to find out someone betrayed you, I'd want to know," I said. "That way, you can move on sooner and not waste any more time on that relationship."

"Before you start to over-analyze what I just told you about Jiff, that is the truth," she said, and added, "You know I can't lie to you, or anyone."

"I know," I said.

"Well, you have the visual gift to see what's off, while I have the audio," she said laughing and we decided to toast and clinked our wine glasses together over my good fortune.

"How old were you when you noticed or could tell when someone was lying?" I asked.

She thought a minute and said, "The first time I knew someone lied to me, I was three years, seven months old, and it was my mother. She said there was a

Santa Claus. I didn't believe her even when she took me to have my picture taken with one. He had a fake beard and I told him so. The next kid in line started crying. We were asked to leave without getting the photo."

"I didn't know there wasn't a Santa Claus until I was six. We were in first grade," I said.

"I know. I told you. I couldn't let you live the lie," Ava said and laughed. "I could always tell when my mother was lying to everyone, not just me. My world was small back then."

By the time we were in second grade, Ava knew when anyone else was lying. from kids who came over for playdates, nurses in waiting rooms, or friends of my mother who didn't want to do something with her.

I said, "Yeah, I could tell when my mother was lying to me cuz her lips were moving. Anything she ever said never benefited me, only my sister."

Only if someone asked Ava point blank, *do you think they are lying?* would she answer truthfully because…she could not lie.

Ava said, "The older I got, the more I thought this was a gift, until I realized the implications of knowing all these lies. What a curse! As soon as I was interested in a boy, and he lied to me—which was usually within the first five minutes of speaking to him—I was turned off to the point I wanted to rip his head off and use it for a bowling ball. Can't any male, young or old, go five minutes without telling a fib? Even if it was a fib, a small white lie as my mother used to call them, it turned me off to them, permanently."

"Remember the Catechism class we were both in? It was second grade. The nuns used a book that showed milk bottles that were white, black or with smudges of black on them. The white ones were pure, no sins, or lies, and the black ones, well, you can figure that out. The bottles with the smudges were what they focused on. The nuns said these were little white lies people told, and thus, made them venial sins, not the black mortal sins in the other milk containers," I said. "I had to ask, if they are small white lies, and venial sins, then why are they smudging the milk bottles with black?"

"You were sent to the principal's office to think about it," Ava said. "Sister Imelda had the personality of a Hun who liked to eat small children."

"Well, she had no answer for me, so she was annoyed. She told me I was there to think about it and to try to figure it out, only I wasn't trying to figure it out. It made no sense and I told her so. She expelled me for a week and called my mother to come get me."

"That's when they moved us from the same classroom to different teachers," Ava said. "Like that would stop our friendship. They thought we were demon seeds. I had no one to share who was telling lies in the classroom. Do you remember our secret sign?"

"Of course," I said. "You touch your neck or necklace."

We heard the elevator ping meaning someone was

coming to the condo. Jiff walked out into the living room where we were sitting, greeting us with a big smile. "Well, do you like it?" he asked. "I know it's a bit masculine with the dark leather furniture."

"I think this place is way too nice for me. Are you sure you don't mind me staying here?"

"NO!" we both answered Ava. It was starting to feel good when we both were in sync as a couple.

"Don't be silly," Jiff said. "If my dog, Isabella, didn't mess it up, how could you?"

Ava smiled and asked, "When can I move in? All I have with me are clothes at this point. I'll leave my furniture in storage until I find my own place."

"Today, tonight, tomorrow, anytime you want. Here's a set of keys and you met Sam, right?"

Ava nodded taking the keys.

"Well, it's all yours," Jiff said. "I'll get a glass of wine and join you. Anyone need a refill?"

Once we were all situated and our glasses topped off, I brought Jiff up to date on the findings at the vet.

"There is some precedence using animal DNA when there is no human DNA," he said.

"Yes, but there could be human DNA that Dr. Kevin got from the dog's teeth and a few fibers of the guy's black hoodie. I saw what the guy was wearing and both of us saw the dog hanging on his arm," I said.

"If the police find the guy wearing that hoodie, I bet the piece that's missing will fit what Volker had in his teeth," Ava said.

"It's a matter of finding a witness who knew those

guys," I said. "Ava, I have an idea. Aren't you going to help Detective Taylor if he takes Volker to foster?"

"Well, yeah, if he calls me."

"Oh, he's going to call you. We might need to convince him to take Volker for walks in that neighborhood. I bet that dog remembers who those two are that broke in," I said.

"That's dangerous," Jiff said.

"Anybody have a better idea?" I asked.

"LET THE POLICE HANDLE IT," Ava and Jiff said in unison.

"That's just it. The police will be handling it, walking Volker," I said. "We'll just tag along to make sure Taylor doesn't have any fostering questions or miss the tell the dog makes when he sniffs out one of those gunmen," I said. "Someone shot that dog, and I want them to pay for it. I'll find them on my own if I have to."

"Think about what you're getting into," Jiff said, his voice in resignation making an exaggerated exhale, then taking a sip of his wine while rolling his eyes at Ava over the rim. Ava saw him and smiled.

"Okay, I'm in," Ava said, a tad bit reluctantly.

I knew Ava wouldn't resist a little caper. She was a good sport and I had great expectations regarding her help.

"I'm sure Volker will tell us something there," I said.

"He's going to tell you to stay out of that neighborhood," Jiff said.

Chapter Nine

Sunday

AVA'S PRIMARY TASK over the weekend was to call Taylor to inquire if he found out where Volker could stay, while I called Dante to ask if the dog could be left at the kennel or if I, or someone responsible, could foster him. Our secondary assignment was to see if the police had any witnesses or suspects in the shooting.

"I thought Hanky and Taylor told you to stay out of this," Dante said after he realized why I was calling.

"They did, but you know, I won't. So, before we indulge in our age-old argument, I have to talk to you about something that happened before you were injured and spent four weeks in a coma."

"What injury? What coma?" he asked in a monotone.

"Funny...I know you remember," I said. "You remember to tell me to stay out of crime scenes. You offered to see if your friend at the Napoleon House, who you said owed you a big favor, would make the upstairs available to me for my wedding. Do you remember that?"

"Yes, but I never got a chance to talk to him," Dante said, "at least I don't think I did."

"You did talk to him according to Taylor. You talked to him on the way to that crime scene to find those guys who were responsible for those young people they were labor trafficking, remember? One of them ran over you in a car. You never got the chance to tell me. Taylor said you did get your friend to let us use the room, and you were pretty happy to be able to get it for us," I said. "I wasn't going to call them or move forward with our plans until you…until you could tell me yourself."

"Brandy, if I did it and Taylor told you, then you should have called them. I'm sorry if I held you up. That was never my intent," he said.

"Taylor said you called him on your way to the crime scene and after that, you didn't tell me because you were in a coma. I think that entitles you to a pass. I just couldn't move forward until you came out of it…until we talked. And you didn't hold us up. The pandemic hitting when it did caused the delay," I said. "You know, no large gatherings…everybody has to wear a mask…stand six feet apart. We'd need a wide-angle lens just to get a photo of the two of us in one wedding photo. Forget the group family photo."

"So, you're not married, yet?" Dante asked, and for some reason in a very long time, I felt I had his full attention.

"No, not yet."

"Have you rescheduled or found someplace else?"

"No, and with current rules regarding the size of congregating, we're probably going to get his mother, the judge, to perform a civil ceremony just to move forward. We're living together and you can imagine how popular that is with my parents," I said.

"Will I be invited? I want the opportunity to speak out when the priest asks if there's anyone who knows why the couple shouldn't be married," he said.

"Now, why would you speak out? After all these years, you had plenty of time to say whatever you wanted or needed to say," I said.

"I'd say I still love you, and I wish it was me," he said.

Stunned silence.

"I really thought we were moving along past this. I'm sorry…"

"It's not your fault. It's mine for not acting sooner, for not speaking up all the times I had the chance. I had plenty of time to think about it while I was at my mother's recovering."

"You were at your mother's house recovering for one day, maybe two," I said.

"That was long enough to review my shortcomings. I want you to know, I'm sorry. I hope you will be very happy with old, what's his name."

"You should forever hold your peace," I said to him. "Well, this ceremony is going to be very small. So small, I'm trying to figure out how not to invite my mother. So outside of our parents, and the Judge who is Jiff's mother...his name is Jiff Heinkel by the way, it will be uber small. We'll have a reception later when this pandemic stuff is over, and we can act normal again. I'll invite you to that."

"Hmmm," he said, and I wondered if he was starting to work on something else. Then to change the subject, I asked, "Um... so, what about that poor dog? He's still at the vet recovering from a bullet through his chest. I can't believe he lived, and he might be the only witness who can prove who the gunmen are," I said.

"What do you mean the dog can prove who the gunmen are?"

"I was hoping maybe I could foster him or maybe get someone in the department to foster him. I hate to see him sitting in a kennel 24/7," I was trying to sound as pitiful as possible. "He'll just get depressed and maybe even die from depression if he has to sit in a crate until the trial."

"What trial? Why is he sitting in a crate...at a shelter?" asked Dante. "Go back to telling me how the dog can prove who the gunmen are, please."

"Because the vet found tissue and fabric in his teeth along with gunshot residue in his muzzle. He collected it during the surgery and gave it to Detective Taylor," I said. "I might add that it was my idea to ask the vets to do that."

"Evidence has to go through a chain of command,"

he said.

"That's why I met Detective Taylor at the vet's office so he could collect it directly from the vet who had called Animal Control when they got a dog into their clinic who had a gunshot wound. He witnessed the transfer of evidence, and he probably took it into custody. And, if there is dog saliva or his blood on the shooter's clothing, that's evidence to convict since dog DNA is so specific. Did you know there's less than one percent chance, in a billion, it could be from another dog," I said.

No response. The phone line was quiet.

"Are you still there?" I asked.

"Yeah, I have to talk to Taylor," he said and hung up.

"You're welcome Dante," I said to the dial tone. "And I still love you too, just not the same way."

Chapter Ten

Sunday

I T WAS ALMOST noon on Sunday when Taylor called my cell and said the department...that meant Dante...approved of him taking Volker to foster. I told him the vet was open on Sundays from noon to five o'clock. I said I could meet him there today to have Volker released to him. We agreed on two o'clock.

"Oh, I'll call Ava and see if she'd like me to pick her up and go with us," Taylor said.

"Good idea," I said, not surprised. "If you're picking her up, let's meet there in an hour. That will give you time."

"You forget I have the benefit of a police siren," Taylor said.

"Okay, in thirty minutes. See you there."

We met at the vet's office and Volker was released to me. I asked Kelly if anyone had called, namely Nina Perez, to see how Volker was doing.

"Someone called, a lady with a Spanish accent and asked about him. Well, she didn't ask how he was doing, but if no one claimed him would he be put down. I said we'd try to get him into rescue unless the owner came in with documents to claim him," she said.

"She leave her name?" I asked.

"No. Hung up when I asked for it. Excuse me, I've gotta grab the phone," she said as she picked up a ringing line.

When Ava and Taylor arrived, I suggested we go to Taylor's house to help get him settled in and to make sure his house was dog proof.

"You know I just moved into this house from my condo in Manhattan, so I don't have much furniture," Taylor said. "I do have a big yard."

"We're not going there to take photos for *Architectural Digest*," I said. "It's not a good idea to let him run free around your yard until he's finally healed."

"Oh, right," he said.

I was starting to wonder if Taylor fostering Volker was a good idea.

Ava added, "We're going to help you with the dog. I'm sure your home is lovely."

I stifled an eyeroll over Ava's comment. I couldn't imagine Taylor's home being lovely. Neat, nice, comfortable with expensive furniture…but not lovely.

"I don't think this will take long," I said. "I can always give Ava a ride back to her place," I said.

"You mean Jiff's place," Ava said.

Taylor had a puzzled look on his face.

"What place did I pick you up from?" Taylor asked Ava. "I thought that was your new apartment."

"You picked me up from Jiff's condo in The Towers at the Lakefront. It's temporary. Jiff has been so kind as to let me stay at his condo while he and Brandy look for a house. He's living with her," Ava explained and nodded toward me as a smile came over Taylor's face.

We agreed to meet at Taylor's house uptown. He gave me his address. This house of his was one of the uptown Greek Revival mansions that needed some cosmetic work, but it was just the kind of house Jiff and I were looking for.

Taylor's house was on Chestnut Street, right off Jefferson Avenue, in an enclave close to Audubon Park. He let Volker off the leash as soon as we were inside.

"No, no, no, no, no," Ava and I said in unison. We looked at each other and I let her explain.

"Take him to the yard outside and then let him off leash so he knows where he needs to use the bathroom. Otherwise, he might decide here is not off limits."

"Well, I'm glad you're here. I'm sure I'll need some more pointers with him as we go along," Taylor said leading us through his home out to the backyard which was massive and included a side yard with a driveway and garage.

"How did you find this place?" I asked him. "This is what Jiff and I have been looking for—a house uptown just like this."

"My brother turned me on to it through one of his clients. They wanted to sell it. He put us together, and

I bought it. It was never listed," he said.

"Well, I need to talk to your brother," I said.

"I'll take you on a tour after we get Volker settled. The exit to the yard is this way," Taylor said leading us through to the kitchen at the back of the house.

The kitchen door opened into a large back porch complete with a swing, a back and a side yard. Volker had a lot of space to run. Taylor's fence was a wrought iron fence about eight feet high around the house and the yards. Unless Volker was a digger, this yard should keep him secure.

"This will be the hard part," I said to Taylor. "You're going to have to walk him on the leash until they remove his stitches, even around the yard. Don't let him chase a squirrel or anything."

"I can take him for a walk around the neighborhood, too, right?" he asked. "Walking a dog will get me out and see what's around me. I'd like to meet my neighbors. Walking Volker will make me do it."

"He needs to be on a schedule," Ava said. "I'll help you if you're having to work and can't get home to walk or feed him."

"That would really help," Taylor said to Ava. "Let's go in and show me what to feed him. Then I'll take you on the tour."

"How different is this from where you lived in Manhattan," Ava asked as Taylor showed us around.

"My brother and I had brownstones right next to each other. They were each four floors, so I had a lot of room I never used. I'm sure this place is bigger than I need, but I love the architecture. Like the Brownstone, the rooms are spacious, and the ceilings are high which makes it feel a lot bigger."

"Your house is amazing," Ava said, and I seconded it.

"I really want to renovate the kitchen and the master bedroom and bath. There's plenty room to do what I want, it's just finding the time," he said.

"And good workmen," I added.

After we went over everything, we could think of to school Taylor on being a good dog foster parent, I offered to drive Ava back to Jiff's condo. When she took me up on the offer I couldn't tell if Taylor was a little disappointed in Ava leaving but reading him was always tough for me.

We said our goodbyes, and Ava gave her cell number to Travis if he needed help with Volker. He told her he would be calling.

On the ride to Jiff's condo I finally said, "I think you like him. He obviously likes you."

"I do like him," she said.

"But…"

"But, after years of knowing how men are, I'd like to give him a wide berth before I even commit to a date. I'm happy to help him with Volker. It will give me a chance to see how he really is. I do find him a little hard to read, but he seems genuine. At least helping him with Volker will get me out to meet people. Right now, I only go see my dad in the nursing home. Not a big dating pool there."

The indifference in the face she made along with the shrug made me realize she didn't need to take risks in relationships. How nice was that?

"He's a detective. That's why he's hard to read," I said.

"Yeah, even when I met him in New York, I didn't get much from him, but I didn't spend much time in meetings or alone with him," she said.

"I wanted to broach the subject of taking Volker for a walk down Nina Perez's block and watching his reactions to people and places. He might tell us something or he might tell us nothing. It's worth going on a walk with a cop carrying a gun on that street."

"I think you're right," Ava said. "We ought to let Volker get stronger in case he spots the gunmen and goes after them. The dog needs to heal first."

"Right you are," I said. "Let's go take a drive by and see if we spot anything."

"That's a bad idea," Ava said.

"Just because it's a bad idea doesn't mean it won't be a good time," I said, giving her my most wicked smile.

It was a nice Sunday afternoon about three o'clock when we drove down Nina Perez's block. The only thing we did see was a car parked in the side driveway on the other side of Nina's half of the shotgun. It must have been the other tenant's car.

"Ava, please write down this license plate," I said as I read it off to her. "That might be the guy's car who lives on the other side of Nina. You can text it to Detective Taylor and ask him to run the plate. Just say we were passing and thought he might like the number to follow up on. He'll love that."

I pulled up and parked across the street from Nina's home.

"Why are you stopping?" Ava asked.

"I want to talk to the guy who told Taylor he saw us putting the dog in my car. If he saw that, I've got to think he heard the shots and saw more than he's telling the police."

"What makes you think he will tell us?"

"He might tell us because we're not the police," I said. "C'mon."

I was knocking on the front door when Ava caught up with me. I could hear someone moving around inside. After the third time I knocked, a man finally answered. He just opened the door, he didn't say hello, what do you want, nada.

"Hi. Do you remember us?" I asked him. "We're the people who helped the dog who was shot."

No answer, and no look of recognition. Okay, I plowed on.

"I know you remember us because you told the police you saw us helping the dog that got shot. We want to know who might have killed our friend across the street and injured his wife and the dog. Can you tell us that? We don't need to know your name; we just want to know why they wanted to kill those two people."

"I don't know who those two were," he finally said.

Ah, he saw there was two. "But you saw them, two men running from the house and you saw them shoot the dog?"

No answer.

"I didn't see nuttin," he said and slammed the door in our faces.

"Thank you for your help," I said to the door inches away from my nose. Turning to Ava I said, "That went well, don't you think?"

Back in the car I sat there a minute trying to figure out why this guy wouldn't talk to us.

"You know, he was lying, right? He did see something," Ava finally said.

"Yeah, I know he probably saw something," I said.

"No, he definitely saw something. He's lying saying he didn't. I know for sure, but I don't know what it was."

"Well, why would he be lying?" I asked. "Let's think. Maybe he knows the shooters. Maybe he has something to do with sending them there or he's afraid of retaliation."

"I didn't get the 'he was scared' vibe, but more like 'I'm not cooperating' vibe. By telling the police he saw us with the dog, it seems like he's cooperating, but he isn't," Ava said.

"That's a real problem for New Orleans. Here, communities won't talk or work with the police," I said.

"It's everywhere, not just here. How can anyone expect gun violence or crime in neighborhoods to stop?" Ava asked.

"I don't know," I said. "You still have that plate number? I'm calling Detective Taylor and giving it to him and adding what we didn't learn in our brief encounter with whatever his name is." I paused a moment and then added, "You think Nina might have a line on that neighbor? Maybe she could tell us why he isn't being very helpful."

"It's worth a shot," she said. "If you're not busy, let's go see her now."

"All right." I called Taylor's cell and left him a message saying we saw the man who told him we took the dog to the vet. I figured he'd call me back as soon as he lassoed Volker or whatever else he was doing on his day off.

AT THE HOSPITAL, Nina was doing a lot better physically. Emotionally, she was devastated. She looked like she'd been crying since we left. I thought the reality of losing Carlos had finally set in.

"Hey, Nina, how are you doing today? Have they gotten you up to walk around?" Ava asked taking her hand.

I placed the flowers we stopped to get for her on

the bed tray so she could see them.

"They made me get up, but I'm not doing so good. I don't know what I'm going to do without Carlos," she said. She blotted at her eyes, but I didn't see any tears.

"Do you have family here, or a close friend you can stay with for a few days?" I asked.

"The nurses keep asking me that also. Our families are all in Mexico. Carlos and I came on work visas and took the citizenship test. We both passed. We were hoping to help some of our family come here, but this happened before we could," she said and wiped her face. "I called a friend I know from work who said I could stay with her for a while."

"I'm sorry, Nina, but we have to ask you something about a neighbor of yours. Do you recall ever meeting the man directly across the street from you? His front door is painted green," I said.

The terror in her eyes sent a shiver down my spine. Even I could tell she knew him. Finally, she said, "I know who you are talking about. Carlos met him the day we moved in. He came across the street, not really introducing himself, but looking around to see what we had. He looked at what we were moving in rather than at us," Nina said. "He didn't offer to help even when I had to lift one end of our sofa. He could see us struggling. After he left, Carlos said not to trust him or be alone with him."

"Did Carlos mention anything in particular as to

why he said that?" Ava asked.

"No, but the man was vulgar and crude asking where we planned to put all our effing stuff," she said. "Carlos started to introduce us as new neighbors but he just turned and walked off when Carlos extended his hand to shake his."

"What about your neighbor on the other side of the double. Did you ever meet him?" I asked.

"No. Carlos did and told me he's a bartender somewhere in the French Quarter. He works nights so he sleeps in the day," she said.

"Ever see who comes and goes out of his apartment?" I asked.

"We're sleeping when he's coming home from work," she said. "I met his girlfriend. She's Spanish like us."

"So, you've never seen any of his friends or who comes to visit him?"

"A Spanish woman was there a short time and then she moved in with the guy across the street. She told me she was down on her luck with no one to help her. I tried to help her. I gave her a ride to the school where I work, and she got a part time job. She only worked as day labor."

"What is your neighbor's name?" I asked. "The one on the other side of the double from you."

"His name is Jason," Nina said and yawned.

I think we were starting to wear her out.

"What time does your mail come, do you know?" I

asked.

"Why do you want to know that?" Ava asked.

"So, we can go look in his mailbox and find out his last name," I said.

"I know his last name. Our mail gets mixed up with his all the time, His name is Jason Mays."

"Do you know a good time for us to try to catch him home?" I asked.

"He's usually home around 5:30 and he would leave for work around 6:30. Carlos would talk with him on evenings we sat outside after we got home from work at 5:30 and we'd see him leave for his job."

"You just reminded me of your mail. Anyone picking up or checking on your mail or deliveries?" I asked.

"No, I forgot about that."

"Would you mind if we go check on your mail and ask the neighbor to call us and we'll go get it for you until you figure out where you will move to?"

"That would be really great and nice of you," Nina said. "When I get out of here and move in with my friend, I can go check myself."

"I'll bring you a change of address form for you to fill in so the Post Office can start forwarding your mail there for you," I said.

As we left Nina's room and waited at the elevator, Ava asked, "Why are you so interested in her mail all of a sudden?"

"I'm not. I'm interested in that neighbor, and this is a good reason to go there and talk to him. If he calls or sees Nina for any reason and tells her, she won't be caught off-guard. We're legit."

"I wish I had thought of that," Ava said smiling.

As we got into my car leaving the medical complex, I suggested we stop by Julia's Bed and Breakfast, so Ava could check out and pick up her things, so I could take her to Jiff's condo.

She agreed.

"You know that girlfriend of the guy next door just moving in with the guy across the street is puzzling," I said.

Chapter Eleven

Sunday Evening

FRANK STOOD LOOKING at us through the leaded glass door of Julia's Bed and Breakfast wearing what looked like a white hazmat suit that covered his head, gloves up to his elbows, an N95 mask with a face shield. He was holding a giant bottle of sanitizer or disinfectant that was fitted with a spray handle in one hand, a rag hanging out of a pocket, and a roll of paper towels in the other hand. He looked like he was guarding the entrance to a contaminated site.

When he spotted us coming up the walk, he made crazy arm motions at us through the glass and wouldn't open it until we pulled our masks up over our faces. His mask was black with big red lips in sequins looking like they were about to give someone a smooch. Frank was in full pandemic mode. This was not his usual concierge uniform he liked to wear of Palazzo pants, a white silk blouse with his red kitten pumps. He did, however, have on the red kitten pumps. The sequined lips on his mask were the same color as his shoes. All we could see were Frank's eyes that were heavily made up with eyeliner and mascara, a-la-heavy-metal-band, like he normally wears.

"Step back six feet," Frank yelled through the door. He stuck his arm through the opening holding a retractable, handheld tape measure extended to six feet to make sure we complied.

As we did, he squeezed two face shields through the tiny opening he made with the front door and put them right outside. Then he stepped back. After we donned our shields, he let us in keeping the extended tape measure open to six feet so he could continue to maintain the safe distancing.

"Frank, I guess a kiss and a hug are out of the question," I said by way of a greeting as he took an exaggerated giant step back away from us. Frank was the poster child for social distancing. As soon as we got inside, he motioned us over to the salon and then spritzed the doorknobs, the outside glass and the doorbell with the disinfectant on anyplace someone might have touched. We didn't touch anything.

"You know we are exposed, not just to each other, but to everyone you encounter as well. It's exponential in terms of who you might get it from. Are you practicing safe pandemic?" he asked.

Ava and I looked at each other. *Safe pandemic?* Was this a new term I missed being drilled into us on the nightly news or just Frank-speak? I assumed he meant doing all the things we were supposed to be doing, so Ava and I exchanged a look before we both nodded an affirmative.

"Frank, have you been tested?" I asked.

"Yes, and I'm negative…today," he said making a big downward motion with his index fingers to emphasize the moment in time as the immediate present. "The Queen refuses to take the test. She said she won't get near someone who has been exposed to thousands while administering the testing. She doesn't mind shopping or going to the grocery where everyone touches the lemons and avocados….and then, she buys them!"

Even though he was muffled through the N95 mask, I made out what he was saying since he was using larger than life hand and arm motions to make his point.

"How many people are checked in and staying here right now?" I asked.

"Only your friend, Ava," Frank said nodding toward her. "Why are you both here?"

"Well, Ava is staying here. I was hoping to see you and Julia. Have a little interaction with some friends," I said.

"That's the kind of thinking that is going to put you on a ventilator," Frank snapped in a snarky muffled voice.

"We're wearing our masks and staying six feet from you," Ava said.

It was pointless to tell someone who was over the top with fear and worry about catching the virus that we were doing all the necessary safety recommendations like washing hands, avoiding crowds, and safe distancing. I meant, practicing safe pandemic.

"Okay…Ava has found an apartment so she's here to get her things. I'm taking her there," I said. I didn't want Frank to tell Julia that Ava was moving to Jiff's condo and stopping what little in the way of revenue was coming in via my company's expense account. "Is Julia here?"

"No. She insists on grocery shopping daily because she has cabin fever. She won't let Gloria come help with the cleaning, sanitizing or cooking, so I'm the 24/7 slave to the pandemic," he managed to say in one breath while he exhaled as if exhausted. "You don't know how much disinfecting it takes to keep this place safe."

"Well, if no one is here," I started to say.

"It's never done. As soon as I finish, I must start over disinfecting," he screamed through his mask.

"It looks like it takes a lot of effort to move around in that suit. Do you wear it all day?" I asked.

"Of course. You should consider getting one for yourself if you don't want to get this," he answered. "What if it's still here next year at this time? Everyone you will meet will have been exposed or had it."

"How much sanitizing can this require every day? There's only three of you here. When Ava leaves, then it will be two," I said.

"The Queen goes out and brings back contamination from the thousands she comes in proximity too. She doesn't know how to keep six feet from anything. I know she is going to infect me, it's only a matter of time when the virus arrives on the last piece of fruit she squeezes and buys," Frank said. He was now wringing his hands and getting more worked up the more we talked about the virus.

I changed the subject. "Ava, why don't you go get your things together and I'll visit with Frank. Frank, why don't we go sit out on the veranda upstairs?" I asked.

"No, no. It's windy up there and someone could sneeze passing by and it could be flying around waiting to contaminate me," he said now looking anxiously up the stairs as if waiting for a giant virus to sweep down and infect him.

"Okay. Do you want me to go wait in the car?" I asked half in jest.

"That would be best," he said and made a wide berth around me to open the door for me to leave immediately.

"Well, it was good seeing you. Tell Julia I stopped by. And, Frank, stay healthy and try not to over agonize about the virus," I said. "The number of hospitalizations and people on respirators is going down."

FIFTEEN MINUTES WENT by while I waited in the car. When I saw Ava coming down the front steps with her roller suitcase with a bag piled on top of it and another over her shoulder, I popped open the trunk open. She put her bags in, then opened the passenger door, climbing in. I asked her, "How long has he been wearing that get-up he has on today?"

"You mean the hazmat suit?" Ava said. "That's what he was wearing when I checked in a few days ago, so I'm guessing he's been wearing it since the start of the pandemic."

"Well, he looks like he's working at a toxic waste site," I said. "He did personalize his face mask. It is oh-so-Frank. I wonder why he hasn't done anything with the face shield. Frank is all about customizing."

"Yesterday, I saw him putting rhinestones on one face shield and when Julia saw it, she screamed at him to take them off. She told him bacteria stick to rhinestones, so he pulled them all off wearing gloves. He put them on without gloves, in case you were wondering," Ava said laughing. "Julia screamed at him again that he already touched them so why bother with the gloves. That's when Frank started crying. There's so much saga and drama with those two."

"Frank is an acquired taste. He's a great designer and seamstress," I said. "Not great at the concierge job for the guest house, but he is a constant source of entertainment...ours not Julia's."

"He showed me the wedding dress he made for you and some things he made for Julia. Of course, he demanded I not come closer than six feet. He stood on the opposite side of the room so I would not contaminate the clothing. I was so far away that it will be like seeing it for the first time when I see your wedding photos. He's quite the designer. I'd love to get him to make me some suits for work," Ava said.

"He'd have to take your measurements and that means he needs to get within six feet of you…inside of what he's calling the zone of safe pandemic," I said.

"Oh, right. how could I forget," she said giving herself a forehead pop with the palm of her hand.

"Julia keeps tabs on what Frank does for others. He made the wedding dress for me before she found out he was doing it," I said. "Julia did offer me her Bed and Breakfast to use for our wedding and reception, but Frank was over the top with ideas and suggestions. In case you haven't noticed, he's kinda hard to rein in sometimes. Julia is too."

"How bad?"

"He wanted Jiff to ride up on a white horse and he wanted to wear a white tuxedo and walk me down the staircase. I mentioned my father was still alive, and, likely, wanted to have that honor," I said.

"Oh, my. I can see why you graciously declined."

"Neither Frank nor Julia picked up on the gentle hint. The pandemic helped," I said. "I'm probably the only person on the planet who has found something to be thankful to the pandemic for. I used it as an excuse not to have my wedding at Julia's Bed and Breakfast."

Ava started laughing. "You're right, at least the pandemic was good for one thing. After you drop me off at Jiff's, I think I'm going to go see my dad. I can catch an Uber or maybe I'll rent a car since I'll need one to get to work. The Bed and Breakfast was great being on the streetcar line."

"If you aren't tired of my company, I'll take you to see your dad. You can arrange to have a rental car company bring you one at work. Saves you another day," I said.

"That would be great. I know my dad would love to see you. He's very happy you helped get me back here so I can be with him."

"Tomorrow morning I'll pick you up and give you a ride into the office. The department secretary can help arrange a car for you. Just in case you might think of walking to the bus from the condo, you'd have to walk about eight blocks up to Canal Street, catch a bus to the cemeteries and transfer to the streetcar line. It's okay if the weather is nice, but if it's late at night, cold or rainy you will want a car. I'll get you a parking pass tomorrow for the lot we use around the corner. You can come in the back door of the building," I said.

"You know, I'm pretty tired from a full weekend I've had so far. I think I just want to go to Jiff's condo and settle in. After I get a car, I'll go see my dad."

"Well, if you get a car tomorrow, I'm happy to go see your dad with you then," I said.

"Deal."

Chapter Twelve

Monday

MONDAY MORNING, EVERYONE attended a virtual kickoff meeting, and to meet the new team member. With Ava, my team was up to six people in the department.

"Good morning, everyone. This is Ava Frost, who is joining our team. She is transferring here from New York so please welcome her," I said.

A murmur of voices ranging from hello, welcome, to hi there, along with offering virtual fist bumps instead of a handshake to the new gal went around the room. Ava graciously smiled and nodded to all participants. There was one woman, Carol Cantor who was in her fifties that came with the department when I was put in charge of it. She had been here even before the department was started. Carol wore straight skirts that were as wide on her as they were long. She wore them above her chubby knees and wore rings that had several small cut diamonds on each hand. She was always holding files or moving her hands around so one would notice the rings. She said her husband was always bringing home a jewelry surprise. They looked as if they had been bought in one of the mall jewelry outlets that cater to the cost-conscious crowd.

Carol interrupted my 'good morning, let's get the meeting started' talk-with "Why did we add someone to this department?" in a not-so-friendly sort of welcome toward Ava. "I didn't know there was an opening."

"Why? Were you going to offer to do both jobs? You barely do the one you have," Fiona, the group's clerical assistant said. She had an ongoing feud with Carol. She annoyed Carol on a constant basis by addressing memos or writing notes and spelling her name with a K.

"I was going to refer my son for the position if it had been advertised like it's supposed to be," Carol snapped.

"This was an intra-company transfer so advertising the job opening was not required," I said. "Ava has come highly recommended via one of the detectives I know in the New Orleans Police Department's Homicide Division. It also helps that Ava worked for the company in New York doing exactly what we do here so she can hit the ground running. Can we get back to the reason we're having this meeting?"

Ava picked up on the fact that I didn't mention we have known each other and kept in touch since high school. The rest of the meeting went smoothly with assignments of client requests to members of my staff.

When I announced we were adjourned, Carol huffed off while the rest of the group stuck around to talk to Ava.

I heard Ava telling them, "Detective Taylor's brother, who still lives in New York, called and asked him if he knew anyone who could help me transfer to a job here. It helped I'm from New Orleans and working for the company. I went to high school and college here. Small world."

LATER AT LUNCH, Ava and I grabbed a quick bite at Mother's Restaurant on Poydras across the street from work. Mother's is an institution to the downtown worker's lunch hour in operation since 1938. They serve breakfast, lunch and dinner. Breakfast is served all day. While they serve hot meals, to me, their claim to fame is the Debris, a roast beef sandwich made from the bits of meat that are scraped back in the gravy after carving the roast. It is served on French Bread.

The story goes that once, a customer asked for the shavings from the gravy added to his sandwich, the owner said, 'you mean the debris?' and an original Mother's term was coined.

"What are you gonna get at Mother's?" I asked. "I'm thinking of a Debris sandwich."

"I was thinking a shrimp po-boy. What's a Debris?"

I explained so we decided to get what we each wanted and split ours in half to share with each other. A lunch feast to be sure. I knew I would be too full after lunch to eat dinner.

While we waited for our order at one of the tables set six feet away from another, she asked me, "What's the deal with that Carol woman?"

"She's just a pill. Left over from the old guard in the company. She's one that will twist what you tell her to her advantage," I said. "I wish the company would offer another buyout, so she'll retire. I've heard the others call her Carol, the Clueless. Try to have as little to do with her as possible."

"Thanks for the heads up. What happened to you and Dante, if you don't mind me asking?"

"I grew up next door to Dante, remember? Our childhood romance was fueled by both sets of parents who wanted us to get married. It's so old-school New Orleans. Our parents were the ones disappointed when it didn't result in their mutually desired and anticipated wedding. The bottom line on my relationship with Dante is that it was stuck in neutral. Kissing a stranger at a parade made me realize what I was missing in a relationship. That kiss pushed me into the arms of a man I am now going to marry."

"Oh, Dante and I had both come to terms with this, it was our parents who didn't, or rather, who haven't," I said. "And likely never will."

"That's too bad," she said.

"Now, I have to ask. Aren't you going to miss friends you made in New York?"

"I didn't really have many, so I worked a lot, long

hours and weekend," she said.

"Surely those who live in Manhattan go places after work, right?"

"Yes, but it's always bars. I'm over that scene. It's hard to stay friends with some of those women who go to bars. They would meet a guy and then I didn't see them until that relationship went kaput. Or they'd ask me a question on their appearance. While I'd try to be diplomatic, my answer was not always well received. If a co-worker asked, 'Does this make me look fat?' I would answer, 'The other outfit is more flattering. That was usually the end of that friendship.'"

"You are making me feel better after all this time I was not-knowing," I said. "Although, it does make me wonder how many people took advantage of me."

"The big problem with liars and their lies, they must remember what they told someone. Sometimes, they might have to add to it to keep from being found out. Now they've compounded what they have made up. Most people don't have the wherewithal to keep all the lies straight or remember who they told what. So, they get caught in a lie, then must lie some more," she said shaking her head. "It's disgusting."

"Wow, I hadn't thought of it that way. I'm glad I found Jiff. It's like winning the dating lottery," I said. "Wait until you meet his family. He does have a brother or two who might still be single."

"I hate you," Ava said smiling.

"Have you talked to Taylor today to see how

Volker is doing or rather how he is doing with Volker?"

"I called him this morning. He was out investigating, or so he said, but he told me no problems with Volker so far. He was going home to walk him or let him out in his yard at lunchtime," she said looking at her watch. "Well, he should be home now. He told me the dog was slow going up and down steps. He also had problems getting him in and out of the house. That's only three wide, brick steps. He blocked off the steps to the second floor inside so he wouldn't pull out any stitches."

"Well, well, well. A caring guy. I'm glad to hear it. We should wait a few days before asking him to take Volker back to that neighborhood for a walk," I said.

"Yeah, what if he takes off after someone and breaks open his wound? That would be awful after he's made it this far," Ava said. "I'll call Taylor later to see if he needs me to walk him after work, unless he calls me first."

"If he doesn't call, let's go to my apartment for a cocktail out on the veranda and you can visit with Suzanne if she is home. Maybe you can help me decide on a date for the wedding." I said. "Jiff gets home about 7:00 p.m. He may want to go out and eat, and you are welcome to join us."

"I can help you with the date," Ava said as we left the restaurant. "But I'm glad I have a car now. I'll call my dad and do a virtual visit after Jiff gets home. After I find a place of my own, I'm hoping I can move him in with me."

"I'd like to go with you to see him one day this week, okay?" I said.

"The only way we can do that is if they bring him to a window and we just see each other, or I take my tablet and virtual visit so we can talk while he sees me."

"I'll go with you to do a virtual visit while he looks out the window," I said.

"He'd love that. That would be great for me too, because then you can tell me if you think I'm being too zealous wanting to take him to live with me," she said.

"Sure, I'll give you my honest opinion. Hopefully, I can tell from one visit," I told her.

Chapter Thirteen

Monday Evening

MONDAY RIGHT AFTER work I followed Ava in her rental car to the Care Facility to pay a visit to Mr. Frost. We waited outside while Ava called his nurse to set up a video call with him. There was a picnic table on the grounds right under the window of Mr. Frost's room, so we set up Ava's tablet there for our call. The nurse rolled him to a window so he could look out and see Ava and she could see him while they spoke.

"This is so hard to finally get here to be with him and Covid makes us have to visit virtually," she said.

"At least you can see him in the window," I said.

We had left at five o'clock to try to make dinner with him but arrived by dessert…some yellow-colored gelatin type dessert. Her Dad said it had no color and no taste.

Mr. Frost recognized Ava at once, and it took a few minutes to remind him how he knew me, then he broke into a big smile. He kept looking out the window to talk to her instead of via the tablet.

After Ava reminded her dad who I was, he said,

"Oh, yes, I remember you. Your dad and I would go to the grocery together and take you girls. We'd do that to give our wives a break. It was a treat for us since we'd always go to Schwegmann's Giant Supermarket over there in Gentilly. That was the biggest one. It was a bigger than Wal-Mart."

"Mr. Frost, I remember going with my dad, you and Ava to the grocery," I said.

"Your dad and I would put you two in one of those giant shopping carts and you two would ride with those big cup holders right in front where you sat. Our first stop after we got you both in the cart was at the bar inside to get a big beer. It was the biggest beer sold in the city of New Orleans. We'd put our beers in the holders right smack in front of you. Schwegmann has their own brand of beer. It was cheap and it was good. Does your dad still drink it?"

Schwegmann's did in fact have a bar in the grocery that ran the entire length of the store. They served beer in what I believe to be 40-ounce cups that rivaled the ones now served in the French Quarter marketed as BIG ASS BEERS. Their grocery baskets had cup holders for the huge beer cups right in front of the kids' seat. Kids could put their hands in the beer.

Schwegmann's had closed in the 1990s and was replaced by Wal-Marts, Costco's and several other grocery store chains in the greater New Orleans area.

"No, Mr. Frost, my dad drinks red wine now," I said. "He lost the taste for beer once Schwegmann stopped making it."

"Schwegmann's stopped making that good beer? You hear that Anna? Where are we going to get good beer, now?"

Anna was the name of Ava's late mother.

Ava answered, "I'll check around and see if anyone else has it, but you know, we can't bring outside drinks in here."

"Next time your dad goes to Schwegmann's, tell him to give me a call," he said to me.

AS WE LEFT the facility, Ava said, "I don't even have to ask you. He has really declined since I saw him a week ago. I can't take my dad to live with me. Even with this job and better hours, I'll still be gone for nine to ten hours a day. He does have better days, though, when he remembers my mother is dead, and I'm the daughter the whole time of our visit."

"Maybe he's just having a bad day. Why don't you talk to the caregivers?"

"No, he was like this a week ago. He seemed lucid at first, but then he kept calling me Anna, my mother's name, asking me to bring him some do-nuts from Picou's Bakery. You remember the Federal Reserve Bakery?"

"How could I forget? They had the best do-nuts and a cake we used to get when we'd pull an all-nighter in college to study. It was called a Washington Pie."

"That's right. It had to have a million calories. My

mother used to work at Picou's in the summertime when she was in high school. She used to make that cake for us for dessert. The neighborhood was bad back then, but she said not like it had gotten when we were in high school," Ava said. "We used to draw straws to see who would get out of the car to order. We made the boys do it. There was a turntable to put your money on and then the donuts came around. You never had direct contact with inside and the windows all were bullet proof double glass with mesh wire in between."

"Yes, the kind they use in prisons," I said. "All that to keep do-nuts safe.

"Not just their do-nuts but that Washington Pie. I have that pie recipe. My mother taught me how to make it. I'll make it for us one night after work," she said.

"That would be great. Getting back to your dad, you'd need live-in help for at least twelve hours a day, and you'd be the one to take care of him during the night. Does he sleep all night, do you know?"

"No, the nurses told me he's up walking around a lot. He sleeps during the day mostly," she said.

"You can always take him for a weekend here and there, and holidays. I think having him 24/7 would be a second job after all day at the first job. You will be exhausted after a few weeks, not to mention how would you get any relief?"

"I know you're right. I just feel so bad leaving him in that home," she said. "Now that I'm back here I can go visit him several times a week on my way home. or take my lunch and have it with him sometimes."

"It's the nicest care facility in New Orleans," I said. "You're also scheduling an extra sitter at night when he needs it the most. You're being a good daughter."

"I don't feel like that."

"Someone once told me, when you go visit someone in the hospital or nursing home you want to feel better about seeing them. In a hospital, there's a chance they will get better and go home. In a nursing home, they aren't going to get better, just older, and you know when they are in there, they are not ever going home. It's sad." I said.

"You're right," Ava said. "That's exactly how I feel."

We sat at the picnic bench after Ava's call ended with her dad discussing her options when two nursing assistants came out for a break and sat at a table six feet away from us, but close enough to hear their conversation.

They were talking about the recent shooting. When Ava and I realized they were talking about the shooting we witnessed we exchanged a quick look. We sat there quietly to hear what we could learn.

One said to the other, "I talked to Q-Ball. He knows them guys in the news who shot that dog."

"What?" a skinny woman in yellow scrubs with flowers asked.

Wait. What? Q-Ball? Is he out of jail? I wondered.

"Q-Ball said he knows the guy who shot that dog last week over off Carrollton," the large woman in pink scrubs said.

"Who dat? Q-Ball?" the skinny one asked. "You dating Q-Ball? In prison? How do that work?"

"Yeah, he says someone told him who the shooter was. You know dat's not right to shoot a dog," pink scrubs said.

"You can shoot a dog that's attacking you. When did you date Q-Ball?" asked skinny, yellow scrubs. "I thought he was incarcerated."

"He is. He calls me when he gets a call time," said the pink, big one.

A woman who was apparently their supervisor came to the door and waved the two back inside. As they left their table and passed ours, the nurse who knew Q-Ball said she was going to visit him in jail the next day.

"I know that guy, Q-Ball, the one they were talking about," I said to Ava.

"One of them said he's in prison. How do you know someone like him?" Ava asked shaking her head.

"I met him through Jiff, well, really through my old aunt at a…well never mind. Long story," I said. "Suffice it to say, Jiff represented him once for his grandmother as a favor, and well, Q-Ball didn't take the second chance and make the most of it."

"So back in jail, huh?"

"Yep. I need to call Jiff and tell him Q-Ball might have info on those two gunmen that could shorten his sentence," I said.

"Why would you want to shorten his sentence?" she asked, her eyes wide.

"Because he's just not one of those really bad guys. He gets caught up in the middle of bad stuff going on. He doesn't see it coming or know when to remove himself from the situation."

"He doesn't pull the trigger, but he's there holding the bullets," she said.

"Yeah, pretty much. Wait until I tell Jiff. Q Ball was his client a couple of times."

"Third time's a charm?" she asked regarding Q Ball.

"I don't think so. Come over to my apartment for a glass of wine," I said. "I'm halfway between this facility and your condo. Suzanne is off tonight, and she'd love to see you."

"That sounds good," she said. "I'll follow you."

We went to my apartment after the visit with Mr. Frost. Suzanne was home. After a happy reunion seeing Ava, Suzanne joined her for a glass of wine on the front porch while I fed Meaux and Isabella. I joined them as they were catching up. The dogs followed me onto the porch.

"Your dogs are great," Ava said. "I always wanted one, but I worked long hours in Manhattan and with the commute, I had to leave early, got home late, and worked a lot of weekends. There was just no time for a dog and that's not fair to an animal. It's like being in solitary confinement."

"Well, you can always come over and get all the doggie love you need with these two," Suzanne said as Meaux jumped in my lap on the porch swing. Isabella made a plea to Suzanne waiting for her to tap her lap for an invitation to jump up.

"They are pretty well mannered," Ava said.

"At the moment only because you're here. Like kids, they know who to impress," Suzanne said tapping her lap to give Isabella the green light.

"That Giant is going to be a handful. I'm wondering if Nina will be able to handle him when she finally goes home, or if she even wants to," I said.

Ava told Suzanne about Volker getting shot, Taylor fostering him and how small in stature the owner was.

"Sounds like he's found a home," Suzanne said. "Taylor likes dogs, and he can handle him."

"Yeah, but he's in the same situation I had in NYC with a demanding job and never getting home much or on time to keep a dog on a schedule. It's not right to the dog," Ava said. "They need a schedule. I've offered to help Taylor as much as I can when he's not able to get home in time to let him out or go for a walk."

We all nodded.

"You know," Suzanne said, "I bet if you walk Volker around that neighborhood where the crime happened, kids will run out to pet him and you'll find out more from them, than you did from that neighbor."

"That is genius," I said.

"They may know something about who shot the dog. Even if they didn't see it, they hear the adults talking and they aren't shy to spill the beans. Collectively, the kids in the neighborhood always know more than the adults," Suzanne said.

Ava and I nodded, and the light bulb went off in my head. Even if Q-Ball did have something on the shooters, he'd want something in return. The kids are forthcoming.

Ava told us, "Taylor called earlier today and said they have no leads on the case. No one is coming forward or is willing to say who it might be."

"No surprise there," Suzanne said.

"On top of that Taylor told me he found something on another homicide that connected it to the Carlos and Nina Perez shooting," Ava said. "A woman, about in her twenties, was found shot and burned. They have not been able to identify. The interesting fact is she was shot with the same caliber gun that was used on Carlos and Nina. They even ran a dental scan on the unidentified girl. That scan showed work done in another country. The bullet who killed this girl is a match to the ones that shot Carlos and Nina Perez."

"Didn't Nina say she and Carlos moved here from Mexico and were trying to help their family get here also?" I asked.

"That's right," Ava said. "They might have known that girl. Maybe she can I.D. her."

"Since Katrina, the Spanish community here has

grown. It's not as cloistered as it used to be," Suzanne said.

"Oh, someone knows something or saw something. They just aren't talking. Nina and Carlos might have been afraid to come forward if they did know something," I said.

"Who can blame them? Probably too scared to talk for fear they will be next," Suzanne said.

"Hey, I thought we were supposed to help you set a date for your wedding," Ava said.

"Good idea," Suzanne said. "So, when do you want to do it? Didn't Frank say…," she put her hands on her hips and shook her head side to side to imitate Frank…"your dress will be all wrong if you wait until the summer. Even the spring is pushing it."

"Yes, he did," I said. "The date now is out of my control with this virus. I'm ready to go to a Justice of the Peace or have Jiff's mother marry us. I just don't know if I'll feel married if it's not in a church or by a priest."

"Married is married, no matter who performs the ceremony," Ava said. "It sounds like a good plan."

"Yeah, do that soon so your dress will be…exactly right for the time of year," Suzanne said using another Frank imitation.

"He made me a beautiful dress. I should listen to him," I said.

"LISTEN TO FRANK?" both asked at once, their voices at least ten octaves higher than usual.

"Frank has a point, even if it is hard to figure out what that point actually is," I said laughing. "I guess I need to talk to Jiff and his mother to see when she could perform the ceremony."

"Have it at their home on Audubon Place with a photographer and you will have beautiful photos. Do some in black and white. That always makes it look timeless," Suzanne said. "You'll feel married if you have the ceremony in that house."

"Why, is it a big house?" Ava asked.

"Think Governor's Mansion big," Suzanne said. "With a staff to go with it."

"I guess I could have it there and keep it small," I said.

"Small will be the twenty or so Heinkel family, your father, mother, sister and husband, the four Alexanders—that's no friends—and the thirty or so staff to go with it. Your idea of small is still over the safe headcount limit for a meeting in Covid times," Suzanne said laughing.

"Oh, how you exaggerate," I said as if insulted.

"There's not thirty or so staff people there. There's maybe three," I said thinking.

Suzanne gave me the questioning look, tilting her head as if to say 'really'? "Okay, five with the cook and gardener. five when they have a party. It might be years before we can all congregate in groups of fifty or more people due to this virus. Even if we did invite the original guest list, a lot of people are afraid to gather in large numbers. By large number, I mean more than ten. If we ever find a house, Jiff and I could have a reception later, after the pandemic. We could have the reception later at the original venue in the French Quarter that Jiff's family owns if the termites ever vacate the premises. I'm assuming at some point in time, hopefully in my lifetime, we can go somewhere in public without wearing a mask and can stand close enough to someone at a party and toast clinking glasses."

"Yes. That sounds like a reasonable, hopeful plan," Ava said. "You can't put your life or happiness on hold."

"You can keep it small like that, as in only the families," Suzanne said. "And the two of us. I promise I won't get closer than six feet to anyone except the bartender. Even with the families and a very few friends, we are going to look like BBs in a bathtub in that place."

"My mother is family, although with the way she treats me, I truly believe I was left on their doorstep. I'm the oldest. I'm supposed to be her favorite. If I can prove the doorstep theory, do I still have to invite her?"

They both nodded.

Chapter Fourteen

Tuesday

A CAR RENTAL company delivered Ava a car at lunch time. Her plan was to visit her dad after work as often as possible so she could have dinner with him some evenings, if she could get there early enough. They served dinner no later than 5:15 p.m.

Nina called me when she couldn't reach Ava to tell us a friend at the college where she worked offered to let her stay with her until she can find another place to live.

"I can't ask them to take Volker. He is so big and needs so much attention. Can you take him to a shelter for me?"

"My rescue will pay for his vetting and find him a home after the trial. Can he stay with the foster home longer?" I said.

"Oh, well then maybe I can post him on Craigslist to sell him if he has all that done for him," she said.

"What?" I asked. "The vet bill is already over five hundred dollars, and I'm going to have to ask you to reimburse rescue if you want to sell him online. Really,

Nina? This is the dog that saved your life," I said not believing what she was saying.

"Well, I can't worry about him right now anyway. I just miss Carlos so much," she added crying.

"The detective who is working your case is fostering him. Ava and I are helping keep him on a schedule with walks," I said. "He will keep him until we find the suspects, or it goes to trial. If you can't take him back by then, I'll find him a good home. Don't worry about Volker. Take care of yourself."

"I need to find another apartment. The Police have arranged for me to get out of the lease fearing gunmen may return since they know I'm not dead. My landlord agreed."

"That is good news. I think it will be hard for you to go back and live in that house or in that neighborhood," I said and added, "alone."

"I'm not sure I can even take Volker back when I do find another place. Carlos said it was hard to find a place that would take large dogs. I'm not sure what I can afford without Carlos helping with the rent, and I've lost so much work. Do you know who I can contact to help me like you're helping the dog?" she asked.

"Not really, but I'll ask around. I've got to get back to work," I said and hung up. I thought, this was a side of Nina I didn't expect.

Jiff met me at home. I told him Ava left to visit her dad, so we decided to go to one of our favorite restaurants to sit outside. We tried to give as many restaurants as we could our business during this time of the pandemic. Restaurants, and those trying to make a living working at them, were all hurting.

Once we were seated at our table and could take off our masks, I mentioned what I had heard at the nursing home when we visited Ava's dad regarding Q-Ball.

"He has used up his last get out of jail free card with me, and his grandmother, I can tell you that," he said. "Q-Ball's grandmother used up most of her savings the last two times I helped him because she asked me, correction…begged me to represent him. Give the info to the police and let them deal with Q-Ball."

"Okay," I said. "I'll call or have Ava call Taylor tomorrow. He'll like to hear it from her."

Our meal arrived, and we had our wine glasses refilled so we could toast our wedding finally moving forward.

After we settled into our meal I said, "One other thing and I can stop talking about the shooting. This gal Nina, there's something cavalier about how she feels toward the dog that saved her life. She asked if I'd take him to the shelter. When I said rescue was paying for his vet bill, she said she could sell him on Craigslist! Granted she says it was her husband's dog, but something's off with her."

"Not everyone treats animals like we do. We're more the exception than the rule. We treat our dogs like they are part of the family. Not everyone feels the same," he said. "Go with your gut. It's always been right-on so far."

During dinner, I asked him what he thought about having our wedding at his parents' house with his mother presiding. I added we should have it soon. "When all the mandated pandemic/virus protocols are a distant memory—like the second after they are lifted— we can plan a big party in our new house."

"Great idea," he said taking my hand across the table. "I'll call my mother and ask if she has a certain Saturday on a weekend—a weekend soon, very soon— that works for her. My calendar is open due to this pandemic so I'm guessing hers is too."

"I have the dress," I said.

"We've already selected everything we wanted with the caterer, the florist and the photographer we were going to use. They should have our choices already on file," Jiff said.

"I had already picked out everything with your mother so it should only take them time to get it ready and adjust the food order for a smaller guest list. The photographer might be the problem on short notice," I said.

"No, it won't. We'll ask my sister. It's been a hobby of hers for years. She loves taking photos of family gatherings and parties. She's quite good at it. I tease her by calling her Ansel Adams."

"Let's just ask your sister since it will eliminate one

person who doesn't need to be there. We can ask her to get the caterer to take any family photo we want her in."

"She doesn't even need to ask anyone. She has a tripod with a remote, and every piece of tricked out photography equipment on the market. Don't worry about that."

"We should just have our family, your best man, and my maid of honor. I just need a witness so maybe my sister or one of your brother's wives or girlfriends could stand for me. Is that okay with you?"

"Anything you want is okay with me. I think you should ask a couple of friends just to even out the attendees. My side of the aisle is going to be packed and your side will be a little light in numbers."

"Well, I would like to have Ava and Suzanne but it's not necessary," I said.

"I'm just glad we're moving forward with this again. For a while I thought you changed your mind," he said tenderly holding my hand and rubbing it.

"No, I never changed my mind or even had the slightest hesitation. We've had a series of unfortunate events that have derailed our original plan. This is simpler, and I like it better. Let's try to keep it as small as possible with the pandemic craze still going on. My only hope is for my mother to have other plans that day and can't make it, but my dad can."

"You don't mean that?"

"I do."

"Get used to saying that!' He called our waiter over and paid the bill. On the way to the car, he hugged and kissed me.

"Let's call my parents when we get home," Jiff said. "They will be ecstatic."

Jiff's parents were elated to have the wedding at their home, and his mother was thrilled to be asked to officiate. Any Saturday was fine with them. Jiff wanted to schedule it this coming Saturday, like in five days, but his mother and I talked him into the following Saturday so that we could make sure the flowers would be there, the food, and if his sister was available for the photos. His mother suggested we go to a studio and have a professional, not that his sister wasn't professional, but a studio portrait made because she wanted one for their stairway wall. All the married siblings including his mother and father had a 24 x 36-inch gold framed photo of their wedding day hung prominently going up the staircase wall.

"Brandy, you'll want your hair done and makeup like you want to wear it for your wedding day. Maybe you could do that this Saturday. Just a suggestion," his mother said.

"That is a great idea. Thank you for agreeing to officiate and open your home to us."

"Don't be silly. You're family now. This is your home, too" his mother said.

His dad chimed in and said, "What about, not this Saturday, but the following Saturday? We'll have whatever you want by way of a post ceremony event."

Jiff suggested we have a dinner for all of us since it might be the only time both families will be together, and his parents agreed. I wondered did he realize by both families that meant my mother would be there also.

I looked at Jiff and said, "Okay, not this Saturday, but the following," letting it sink in.

He nodded in agreement and we were both beaming from ear to ear at each other.

"My parents are ecstatic," Jiff said after we hung up with them. "Maybe you couldn't tell, but I could."

I CALLED MY parents. When my dad answered, I told him first. I asked him to tell my mother. He was happy for me setting the date, but he wanted me to talk to my mother.

Why???? I asked myself. His voice was muffled as if he was holding the phone against his shoulder to talk to her. Before he could put her on the phone, I hurriedly added, "I'm getting married next Saturday. Jiff's mother is a judge, and she will officiate at her home. They live on Audubon Place, and we will have a small, I mean only family, celebration with food and cake following. The only guests are Jiff's family, you, Mother, Sherry and her husband. That's it," I said.

My dad was repeating what I told him to her. I guess she didn't want to talk to me either.

"What do I have to wear?" I could hear my mother

asking in the background. Now, I was sure my dad was holding the phone between them so they could both hear me.

"Tell Mom to wear something nice. Jiff's parents live on Audubon Place, you know the private street off St. Charles with the guard shack. That's where we're having the ceremony. It's the very large, white home with marble steps and big columns right on the corner.

"When you pull up there, tell them you are going to the Heinkel wedding. They will have your name on a list," I said. "Be there for 4:00 p.m., not this Saturday, but next. After our vows we will have a sit-down dinner and cake," I said.

"I don't know if I can find something nice enough to wear to their very large house with the big columns on Audubon Place by next Saturday," my mother was saying in a snarky tone thinking I couldn't hear her.

"If Mom can't make it, she can't make it. Dad you will be there, right?"

"Yes," he said after a slight hesitation which I'm sure involved checking out any look my mother was sending him.

"If she doesn't want to come, don't force her. I'll make up a good excuse they will believe, like you finally had her committed to a mental institution and they took her away in a strait jacket an hour before the wedding. Oh, well."

"Brandy," he said in the tone of voice he used when he wanted me to make the effort to get along with my mother. Little did he know this was me getting along with her.

"I do want you there, please. Just wear a suit and tie. These people are very nice," I said.

"You think I should wear a tuxedo?" he asked.

"You know that would be grand," I said. "You'll look very nice in the photos whatever you wear. I'm sure Mr. Heinkel and all of Jiff's brothers will all be wearing tuxedoes, so if you think you'll feel more comfortable wearing one, then, please do."

"Yes, I'll wear a tux," he said sort of absent mindedly. I'm sure he was wondering how much that was going to cost to rent. I'm sure my mother was thinking of ways to talk him out of it.

"Thanks, Dad. Be there by 3:45 p.m. Remember, not this Saturday, but the one after. The ceremony starts at 4:00. Plan to stay for dinner and cake," I said. "The whole event should last about two hours."

"Sure, honey. We'll be there," he said. "I'm happy for you."

I wasn't sure if he meant, he will be there, or, we will be there, including my mother. She had a lot to think about, especially if it meant she would be left out. I knew she would come because, how else could she rail on me about what wasn't right about my wedding for the rest of her life?

I called my sister and told her when and where our ceremony would be. She asked if she could bring the twins. Oh God, no, I thought. I said, "I'm wondering if that is a good idea for them. It should only last about two hours. It might be best to leave them with Dante's mother. I think that would be safer for the babies, don't you think? I'm worried they could catch something and have to go to a hospital with the pandemic right now."

Anytime a suggestion put her twins' needs, and thereby hers, first, my sister would agree to. It made her feel like the center of the universe. My luck was holding out. She agreed to ask Dante's mother and said it was a good idea to leave them with her. She even asked if I wanted her to ask our mother to watch them.

"If you think you can get her to do that, I'd be eternally grateful, but don't push it," I said. "I want Dad there. Call me the minute it sounds like she is trying to keep him from coming."

"Will do. But I can't promise anything. I'm happy for you," Sherry said and we hung up.

Chapter Fifteen

Wednesday

I woke up wondering if Q-Ball knew who shot Carlos and Nina's dog, then he knew who shot Carlos and Nina. It's a small world in certain New Orleans circles, and the crime circle, with as much crime that was here, was amazingly small. Kingpins came and went, but everyone knew who the new ones were.

On the drive into the office, I made a call to Dante to tell him about the conversation we overheard. It seems Ava had already told Taylor what the two nurses were talking about, and he had relayed it to Dante.

"Q-Ball is a weird one, I'll admit. He does seem to know or hear things and he's easily manipulated since he really isn't a hardened criminal," I said.

"He isn't? Then, what's he doing in Parish Prison?" Dante asked. "If his stay there doesn't make him a career criminal nothing will."

"Can we get in there to talk to him?" I asked.

"Are you crazy? Why would I send you into that cesspool of human deviants? That's what their lawyers are supposed to do."

"Dante, he might know who shot Nina, their dog and killed her husband."

"Then my detectives will talk to him and find out what he knows or what he's willing to trade for. You can't offer him anything," he said.

"I could ask Jiff to represent him," I said.

"I doubt that is going to happen. This Q-Ball is a big loser with no money to pay an attorney. He's lucky he has a public defender who might, I repeat, might get him a deal if he has good information on these shooters."

I was so annoyed with Dante, I hung up on him. It felt terrible, so I called him back.

"Deedler, Homicide," he answered.

"Goodbye!" I said and hung up.

After I made the first call to the event planner at the Heinkel's building in the French Quarter that was still undergoing repairs from the termite damage, she asked if I wanted any changes other than to downsize the guest list and I said no. Our event planner said she would contact the caterer, florist, bakery for the wedding cake, and give them the new date and make any changes to the orders.

I told her I still wanted a three-tier wedding cake but smaller tiers. I just wanted it to look tall. Whatever was left over I'd like it sent to Mr. Frost and friends at the nursing home.

She suggested what she thought should be scaled

down saying she knew exactly how the Heinkel's liked an event in their home. She would arrange for the appropriate number of waiters, servers, and a butler to greet guests at the door.

"There will only be my parents, my sister with her husband, and two of my friends," I said. "All the rest will be Heinkels."

"Well, there's the officiate or whoever they have asked," she said. "Even if there's only one guest coming for dinner, this is what the Heinkels have me arrange. Don't worry. It will all be splendid for your big day."

Oh my! I thought. A butler? Now, I was hoping my mother would show up. I thought having a butler open the door and announce her was going to throw her totally off guard and make her self-conscious for at least the two hours our wedding and dinner would take. Maybe they wouldn't even stay for dinner. What am I thinking? My dad will get along fine with them and want to stay and eat with us.

My dad was the kind that would fit right in at their mansion or in a bowling alley. My mother would look down on those in a bowling alley. She was about to see how bowlers felt when she showed up at the Heinkels, not by my future in-laws, but by the sheer magnitude of their home and their elegant behavior. Maybe it would keep her from saying anything embarrassing. The worse I figured she would say would be to bring up the chance she gave me at getting married in church when my sister married Dane's brother. Of course, she might have to mention it was so I could marry Dante, even though he hadn't asked me. Oh well, the Heinkel's were gracious enough to handle anything she would blurt out.

With my wedding in less than two weeks, Ava and I didn't have much time to figure out how to find the two gunmen who shot up Carlos and Nina Perez. A lot of my time was free now that I didn't have to re-invent my wedding plans.

After making the short phone call to the event planner the wedding was set. I felt like there was more I should be doing. I made a call to the photography studio who had done all the family wedding portraits in the Heinkel home. When I mentioned it was for me and Jiff Heinkel, he asked when I wanted to come in. I told him Saturday, and we agreed on a time in the morning.

I called to make an appointment for my hair and asked Jeffrey if she had someone she could suggest for my makeup.

"Yes, of course I can find you someone. Me!" she said hardly able to contain her enthusiasm. "I do makeup for brides all the time. I'd be thrilled if you let me do yours. When is the wedding?"

"This Saturday we're having a portrait photo done at 11:00 a.m. and the following Saturday is the wedding. I need you on both of those days," I said.

"Okay, this Saturday come in early, like 9:00 a.m. That gives us plenty of time and you can enjoy it without rushing. I'll even have champagne for us to celebrate."

"Remember, I must make it through the day with other errands. You couldn't make this be any easier for me. Thanks," I said. "This makes me have one stop for both!"

"Now, your wedding day. I can come to your house first or wherever you are having the ceremony and help you get dressed. What do you prefer?"

"Well, let's do my makeup and hair at my apartment. Jiff will be at his parents' home that day. Our ceremony is very small due to the pandemic. We're keeping it to family only. Unfortunately, my mother takes up an invitation where I'd rather have a friend," I said.

"Times are what they are. This is your day, so you should do it the way you want. Girlfriend, I'll see you at 9:00 a.m. on Saturday."

Everything was rolling right along. Now, I had to figure out if Volker could identify the shooter of Carlos and Nina. I felt a little guilty for being so happy with my upcoming wedding when their world had been shattered. I wanted to help them. even if Nina wasn't a role model for responsible pet ownership.

My mind wandered back to how could Q-Ball, in jail, know who shot Volker?

I met Q-Ball's grandmother when Jiff was representing him and trying to get him out of jail once before. I also remembered where she lived. I hoped she might remember me.

I decided to pay her a little visit. The lady was sharp and remembered me the instant she opened her door. I didn't even need to pull down my mask and show my entire face.

"Hello, Miss Balsor, remember me?" I asked.

"Of course, I do. Please, I think I asked you to call me Grady. Did Mr. Heinkel come with you?" she asked.

"No. I'm here on my own," I said.

"Please come in." She stood aside to allow me to enter and showed me to a nice sofa in her small living room. As I looked around, I could see every surface had either a family picture in a frame or a knick-knack took up residence. It was also spotless.

"You have a lovely home." I looked around the living room. "Everything is so well organized," I said looking at her family photos in nicely arranged groupings.

"I spent forty years cleaning houses, and now I just clean my own," she said. "I know you didn't come here to ask me housekeeping questions."

I smiled.

"How is Mr. Heinkel. Aren't you two getting married?"

"Yes, we are and it's going to be soon, but we got delayed with the pandemic. I'm sorry to tell you, but he doesn't want to get involved with representing your grandson again," I tried to tell her with all the empathy

I could muster.

"Can't blame him," she said. "I get a phone call every other day from him asking for money. He never asks how I'm doing. I went through all my savings trying to help him the last two times he was in jail. He's gonna get a shock when I die, and he finds out there's nothing left." She took a seat in an armchair across from me chuckling to herself.

I sat down giving her a soft smile.

"What can I help you with?"

"I'd like it if Q-Ball would call me because I think he knows something about a crime that I witnessed, and I'm hoping he can help me get justice for the woman who was shot and her husband who was killed."

"Oh Lord, don't tell me he's now mixed up in a double murder," she wailed.

"No, no, no, no. I'm sorry if it sounded like that. I overheard two women talking in an elevator at a nursing home when I was visiting someone. One lady, a nurse, I think, said Q-Ball told her he knew who shot their dog, also a victim at that same shooting. I'm hoping he knows who shot the dog, because that's who shot the people," I said.

"I'll ask him for you. I'll tell him I heard these two talking. He's more likely to tell me. He always figures I'll never give him up," she said.

"Well, I won't give him up either," I said.

"If you ask him and he tells you, he's going to want something. That something might be money or to get

Mr. Jiff to get him outta jail. I'm thinking he'll want the second one since I told him I'm not gonna spend any more money on him. Leave me your number. I'll call you as soon as I hear from him," she said. "It might be a while."

I thanked her and left my number hoping she could get him to tell her who it was.

Chapter Sixteen

Thursday

WHEN AVA CAME into work, I was waiting at her desk. I suggested she talk Taylor into taking Volker for a walk on Saturday afternoon, any time after 3:00 p.m. All my wedding errands will be done, and I suggested she tell Taylor that she and I would go get him for a follow-up vet visit and then talk him into a walk. It was time for his follow-up visit to make sure he was healing like he should be.

It didn't take long for her to call Taylor and set it up. We'd pick up Volker for 3:00 on Saturday. Taylor was having a key made for her so she could get into his house to help with the dog should he not be able to make it home. I was willing to bet Taylor could make it home five minutes after Ava got there.

"Whoa, I have to call the vet and see if they can see him around 3:30 this Saturday." I said.

"I should have a key to his house by then and will be able to get in to get Volker even if Taylor's not there. In fact, I'll tell him I'll walk him on my day off, and that's this Saturday."

"Sounds good. Let me run. I'll call you if that isn't the plan for Saturday," I said. "Otherwise, I'll see you Saturday at 3:00 at Taylor's house."

I WAITED UNTIL Friday before the studio portrait to pick up my dress from Frank. I was dreading having to tell him and Julia that the wedding was taking place at the Heinkel's home and they weren't invited. I hoped Frank was still practicing safe pandemic, if there ever was such a thing.

There was no need for worry. As I walked up to the front door, I could see a dress bag hanging in the foyer on the hall tree through the leaded glass doors. I didn't even need to ring. By the time I reached the top step, I saw movement in all white flickering through the glass prisms making Frank's movement look dance like. He cracked the doors open just wide enough for his rubber-gloved hand to slide through and hand me the dress-bag. Then he closed the door and proceeded to yell at me through the glass.

"I should be there to make sure it looks perfect on you," Frank said from behind the mask and shield on the other side of the door. I could see him waving his arms around through leaded glass trying to convey something only Frank knew at that time. I could not hear him.

Finally, after many tries of telling him something and not hearing his muffled reply, I pulled out my cell phone and called the concierge phone. Now we could see each other and hear each other.

"We are having a reasonably small, family-only wedding," I told him. "I expect about twenty-five people, plus or minus one, with my family and Jiff's. There will be some waiters and servers there. Oh, and the caterer will probably be there for the cake. Would you feel comfortable around that many people not wearing masks?"

"Not wearing masks!! Why ever not??" he screamed from behind his shield and mask.

"Well, for the family photo for one. Standing six feet away from one another might make our wedding photos look like only one person was in attendance. I don't know if the photographer can get Jiff and I in one together if we stand six feet apart. It's family and most of us have only been around each other. We are practicing safe pandemic, as you call it. You know, we'll take one of each. One with masks, and one without. Everyone will respect the zone of safe pandemic."

"It's for your own safety," he said. "I really would love to be there, but I-I-I just can't. You understand, right?"

Thank God, he was clear on this. I thought he knew I wasn't inviting him. "Oh, absolutely. I will miss you, but you will be there when this is all over and we have an event, a party to celebrate sometime down the road...after the pandemic is over."

"It will NEVER be over," he said over the phone in the tone he used when he was being overly dramatic.

What am I saying? Everything Frank said was in a tone of the overly dramatic. I could see him waving his arms around every time he said anything. Finally, I just waved goodbye.

"Frank, pray we get a vaccine sooner than later. Gotta run."

Chapter Seventeen

Saturday

ARLY Saturday morning I met Jeffrey and had a
wonderful time with her blowing out my hair and
playing with her makeup and mine. She brought a
bottle of Moet Chandon and poured us each a glass.
When she finished, she said, "You look fabulous! That
photo will be spectacular."

Jiff's off getting a haircut and is planning to meet
me at the studio. I picked up my dress from Frank
earlier in the week. I all but had to arm wrestle it away
from him," I said to Jeffrey.

"I'm surprised he wants to miss the wedding,"
Jeffrey said.

"He really just wants to miss the corona virus," I
said. "He's crazy over the top with worry he'll be
exposed to it and get it."

"Well, things and illnesses seem to move around in
a circle of friends or those you meet on a regular basis.
You know, the ones you have contact with or know
either superficially, like co-workers or acquaintances
who have something in common. People you see

regularly, even if it isn't social in nature," Jeffrey said. "He might know someone who came down with it."

"Uh…yeah," I answered. Something she said just clicked in my head about the circle of friends or those you see on a regular basis, even if it isn't socially. That struck a nerve with the Nina and Carlos shooting. What was it? Who did they encounter regularly?

I couldn't stop thinking about what Jeffrey said. Something was connected to the Nina shooting. I pondered who we really knew in Carlos and Nina's contacts on the drive over to the photographers. That little thought got pushed to the back of my mind as I pulled up and saw Jiff waiting for me.

Jiff asked me when we met at the photographer's if I was worried about him seeing me in my wedding dress before our big day.

"No, because I don't believe in those types of super-stitions and our wedding is anything but traditional," I said. "Finally, it's all about us."

"You're right," he said.

Our photo shoot went well. It was fun to play around with Jiff, romantically, in the photos. We almost forgot the photographer was there. It was a reconnection we needed after all the setbacks and craziness from the first attempt at setting a date, to the virus that was now wreaking havoc in our lives.

The photographer encouraged us at first, but then, once we relaxed well…we had fun. There was one we selected for Jiff's mother that I could already picture hanging on the wall going up the stairs.

I asked for prints of several we both liked for our wedding album. We looked so happy and calm. No one was there to distract us from each other which could happen after the ceremony at the Heinkel's home…i.e., my mother might be there giving me an unpleasant stare. I'm sure any photos I was going to take with her in proximity was going to capture a stressed look on my face.

Jiff and I changed, and he wanted to take me to lunch. I suggested Croissant d'Or.

"Didn't you and Ava just go there?" Jiff asked.

"Yes, we went there a week ago, but you weren't with us. I forgot how good their croissant sandwiches are. I have had an envie, as the French like to say, for another one. It sounds so much better than I really want another one."

"Yes, it does. Then, let's go there. I must admit since you told me y'all went there, I've had a strong…envie… for one of their croissants too. I almost sent one of the assistants there to pick up lunch for the office last week. I wonder if they have any Apple Strudel, like they make for Oktoberfest."

While we waited for our lunch, Jiff said his sister was thrilled to be asked to take photos at the wedding. She even recommended using a drone to have some ariel shots of the ceremony and guest out on the lawn.

"That is a grand idea," I said. "I was thinking I'd ask her about using a drone for that very idea. It would be a neat perspective looking down on our ceremony in years to come."

"She's already thought of that and more, I'm sure," Jiff said. "She is so happy for us."

We finished our lunch and Jiff ordered some Apple Strudel to take home for our breakfast tomorrow and a box full for his office.

"I have to get in that dress again in a week," I said as Jiff paid and we stood to leave the restaurant.

"By the way, my mother reached out to your parents and asked if there was anything special your mother would like for our big day." Jiff said ever so casually as we started to leave the table.

I stopped in mid-air, halfway between a sitting and a standing position. "No. Tell me she didn't."

"She did, but she meant well. She did it without mentioning to me she planned on calling, or I would have suggested she talk to you first. My mother also wanted to know what color dress your mother was wearing so she wouldn't wear the same. Apparently, that's a big deal between the mothers of the bride and groom," Jiff said taking a step back away from me.

"I'm sure your mother was just being the gracious lady she naturally is, but I can only imagine what my mother answered or told her," I said finding myself sitting back down in the chair because I felt weak in the knees at the thought of that conversation. "Tell me exactly what she said."

"My mother is more than happy over our wedding.

She's ecstatic."

"I know that part. What did my mother say?"

"She got like this whenever one of my brothers got married. It seems she rides a bigger high with every nuptial. She and my dad are thrilled for us, for their son to find happiness in the perfect match." He added, "Her words, not mine. She said she feels like the mother of the bride since our sister looks like there's only a career in her future. No husband and no kids."

"Oh noooooo," I moaned. "This build-up can't be good. Let me start by apologizing first. I'm so sorry for anything…everything…my mother might have said. I need to call your mother immediately and apologize profusely."

"Don't be silly. She said your mother hadn't decided what color to wear and she didn't mind if they both turned up in the same color," Jiff said.

"My mother…if she comes… will be wearing a long black dress with a veiled black hat. She'll look like a beekeeper or like she's going to a funeral," I said.

Jiff helped me to my feet and gave me a hug. "It's going to be a perfect day. You'll see. My mother offered to send the company limo to pick your parents up, so they don't have to worry about having a few celebratory drinks," he said.

"I could send an UBER or a hearse," I said. "Your mother doesn't need to do any more for our wedding than what she's offered and has done so far."

Jiff just shook his head at me with a big smile on

his face. "It's making her happy. Let her do it. You should let yourself enjoy it," he said kissing me on my forehead.

"You're right. I'm going to. Did I ever tell you I feel like I've won the love-lottery finding you?" I said.

"Yes, but you can tell me as many times as you want."

JIFF WENT BACK to his office to catch up on some things, and I went to meet Ava at Taylor's house. She was already there.

It started to drizzle just as I pulled up in front of his house. When I opened the car door, it started to come down in buckets. I sat in my car a few minutes and then decided to call Ava on my cell and talk about the weather.

"Hey, I see you sitting out front," she answered.

"Well, do you have the radar app on your phone? It looks like we're in for a shower for the next few minutes and then it stops. This is going to impact our walk-about with Volker," I said.

"If you don't have an umbrella, I'll come out and get you with mine. Let's wait here a bit and see if the rain stops or slows down," she said.

"OK. Let's give it ten minutes and if it doesn't stop, I do have an umbrella. I'll brave it then," I said hanging up.

New Orleans rain showers often brought street flooding in many areas around town. I wondered what was going to happen on this street and if I'd be able to drive out of the neighborhood in my BMW. I thought my next car might need to be more of a SUV and a lot higher off the ground.

Right then my phone rang, and it was my mother. I hesitated and wondered if I should ignore it, but she never called me, and I had a flash something happened to my dad.

"Yeah, Mom, what is it?" I answered.

"Well, hello to you too, Miss Hoity Toity," she said.

"What's wrong? Is it something with Dad?"

"Your future mother-in-law called me and asked what color I was wearing to the wedding. I'm glad your father told me you were getting married. Imagine my surprise if she was the first one, I heard it from," she said in a most disinterested tone as if she was filing her fingernails while she talked to me.

"I heard you listening and commenting while I was telling Dad. Don't lie, you knew," I said.

No comment. Just nail filing.

"Right. Didn't know Mrs. Heinkel was going to call, but since she is the epitome of grace and good manners, she was thinking of you and wanting you to feel included," I said.

My mother totally missed the fact I was suggesting she should try grace and good manners like Mrs. Heinkel.

"She asked me if I wanted anything special at the

ceremony. I told her I wanted my oldest daughter to get married in a Catholic Church, but you didn't ask me what my wishes were," she said.

I internalized a groan.

"That was rude to say since they are having our ceremony in their home and hosting the dinner. What a great first impression you must've made. You don't have to spend a dime on my wedding, and I thought that should make you happy," I said. "Happy for you. Not happy for me. Wear the dress you wore to Sherry's wedding. The same people who were at her wedding will not be at mine, so no one will notice."

She hung up on me.

I waited for the rain to lighten up with the hope it would stop so we could take Volker on our planned mission. My phone rang again, and I thought it must be my mother calling back with something acidic she forgot to mention. The number was different and Mrs. Grady Balsor's name appeared on my cell phone.

After our hellos, Mrs. Grady told me Quincy (she never used his nickname of Q-Ball) was talking trash and had no info about the shootings. He did hear the rumor but had no name.

"I think he was trying to impress that girl you heard talking about him, like that's the way to do it," she said. "Sorry, but you're wasting your time with him."

I thanked her and thought, another dead end just as the rain stopped.

That's when I got my umbrella out and made a dash for Taylor's front door.

Chapter Eighteen

Saturday Afternoon

I F YOU DON'T like the weather in New Orleans, wait twenty minutes, and it will change. That only pertains to rain vs. no rain. It doesn't mean a thing or apply at all when it comes to the heat and humidity. The rain stopped, but the increase in the humidity must have been 300% since my clothes and hair felt damp. Oh, and if there's a hurricane, all bets are off. That means rain for days with street flooding.

Ava answered Taylor's door and held it open as I shook off the rain and tapped my umbrella outside to eliminate any unnecessary wetness accompanying me into the detective's home. She pointed to an umbrella stand in the corner of the foyer where there were several umbrellas of different colors and sizes. Taylor looked like he had an umbrella fetish.

"C'mon back to the kitchen. We were just feeding Volker," Ava said leading the way.

Taylor was filling a water bowl for Volker when we entered.

"Hey, Alexander. This dog is great. He's smart and

catches on fast to what you want him to do," he said putting down the water bowl near Volker's food bowl. "He's got a good appetite."

"I called and spoke to Dr. Kevin, you remember him at the vet's office, for a Volker update. He said it's okay for Volker to go for longer walks but he must stay on the leash. He can't strain or chase anything."

"Look at this weather. Did the vet say he needs to wear a raincoat, carry an umbrella, wear galoshes?" Taylor asked.

"Do you want me to call him back and ask?" I said. The two lovebirds thought that was hilariously funny.

"This might be too wet a day to take Volker for a walk," Taylor said. "He's just starting to feel better and has more energy. What if he catches a cold in his condition?"

"I think you might just be the best foster dad I've ever placed a rescue with. How can I clone you?" I said. "You know, you just said he's eating well and moving around much better, right? The idea is to try to get kids in the neighborhood to come up to pet him so we can ask them some questions, right?" I asked. "It's stopped raining and by the time we get there, this heat will have the streets and sidewalks dry. It's eighty degrees outside."

"It might work. In New York when I was under-cover, the kids always knew who the cops and the bad guys were. Often, they also knew where we all were." Taylor paused a minute tapping his pen on the kitchen counter thinking. Finally, he said, "That's actually a pretty good idea. Then, let's go. Alexander, you drive. I don't want a wet dog in my car."

"But a wet dog can run all through his house," Ava said to me as we got together our raingear.

The part of town that the shooting happened in was not far from Taylor's address, but in an entirely different neighborhood. Neighborhoods changed drastically just by crossing a main street like St. Charles Avenue or Claiborne Avenue, once prestigious thoroughfares in the city.

Taylor's side of St. Charles was considered Uptown while the other side of Carrollton Avenue fell into the Central City locale.

Once we parked, and got out with Volker, we—meaning Ava and I leaving Taylor to wait in the car out of sight. Too many of the residents got a good look at him the day of the shooting when he went door to door. He was, officially, our backup and lookout.

"Your job, should you decide to take it, will be to render assistance if we get in trouble," I said with Ava nodding.

"Just don't provoke anyone to shoot at you. I'd hate to have to tell Dante you got shot on my watch. It will seriously impact my pending promotion," he said.

"I'll work that into our plan," I said and shut the car door.

We left the car and sauntered up the street on the same side Carlos and Nina lived on. Volker started a slow growl when we were three houses away from his home. He was looking across the street at something. A house, maybe? We couldn't figure it out.

"Let's walk back on that side," I said to Ava. She nodded.

Three kids were riding bikes in the street. One kid yelled out, "Is that the dog that got shot?"

"Yes," Ava answered. We had agreed she'd be the spokesperson in order to ask the right questions to see if someone was lying.

"Why are you bringing him back here?" the kid on the bike started circling in the street alongside of us. "The owners got shot too. They are dead."

We didn't see the value in telling the neighborhood pipeline that Nina Perez was still alive for fear it would bring her harm. The boy on the bike was joined by another two riding in the opposite direction but were also curious about the dog.

"He's recovering and he looked depressed," Ava said. "We thought it would make him happy if he got to walk around in his old neighborhood."

"We never saw him walking around here," one kid said.

"Really?" Ava said. "He's real friendly if you want to pet him."

The kids dropped their bikes and came running over.

"You need to approach him slowly and carefully because he doesn't know you," I said.

"Let him smell your hand like this," Ava said showing them to hold the back of their hand out.

The kids did as they were told. "Do you know who shot him?" asked the first kid who noticed us.

"No, but we'd like to find out. That was a terrible thing to do to an animal," Ava said. "Don't you think?"

"I don't know. He was attacking one of those guys," the kid said.

"He was protecting his family. Did any of you see him attack the man?" Ava asked.

"No," said the first kid who stopped while the other two shook their heads.

"So how do you know he did?" she asked.

One of the other kids volunteered, "That kid that's always home studying saw some guy shoot him while he was looking out his window. He's always sitting in the window to study."

"What kid?" Ava asked. "What house does he live in?"

"That house on the corner. He lives with his parents," one kid said.

"Yeah. He's really good in school."

"You all go to school together?" Ava asked.

"Yeah, that kid is the smartest kid in class," one boy said.

"We just ask him if we want to know who did what," said another kid on a nice new bike. "I sit behind him in school."

"Show us where he lives, please," Ava asked.

"What about the man who lives in that house with the green door?" Ava asked. "He said he saw us take the dog, but he didn't see the two men with the guns who shot the dog."

"The kid in the window might know. His name is Clarence. He watches and he hears his parents talking when he's supposed to be asleep. His dad is afraid of guy in the house with the green door," the first kid who rode up said. "Clarence told us."

"What about your parents? Are they afraid of him?"

One kid said, "I live with my Grandma. My mother was arrested for drugs. She be in prison, so now I live with Grandma. She told me to stay away from that man. I don't know why, but I'm more afraid of my Grandma than him, so I listen to her."

"That's right. You should listen to your Grandma. She wants what's best for you, because she loves you," Ava said.

"I don't know about that," the kid said laughing at his own joke.

"I don't know nuttin' about him," one of the other kids said. "My mother works all the time, cuz I got no dad. He got shot on this block over a drug deal."

Now it was clear with the common drug theme why Nina and Carlos were victims in this neighborhood, even if it was accidental.

The kids rode off when they had their fill of petting the dog or answering our questions. If I wound up on future crimes scenes, I needed to remember to make friends with the neighborhood kids. They were a pipeline of information.

We decided to talk to the kid in the window. We strolled at a slow pace past his house. There was a boy, eight or nine years old, wearing black frame eyeglasses, sitting in the window looking out. He was holding a book.

I waved at him and beckoned him to come out. He pointed at himself to make sure I meant him. He left his post in the window and came to the front door. He opened the door only as far as the safety chain would allow to talk to us.

"Our dog is really thirsty," I said. "Do you have a water hose somewhere outside of your house we could use to give him a drink?"

He must have decided we were safe. He opened the chain and came outside and down the steps waving us to follow him to the side of his house. "Yeah. There's a hose you can use around the side of the house," he said as we followed him.

We stood along the side of his house where the faucet was. The boy turned it on and handed the hose to Ava. We stayed on the side of the house, out of sight of anyone on the street and Taylor sitting in my car. Volker drank from the hose.

"Thanks," Ava said. "I'm Ava and this is Brandy. What's your name?"

"Clarence," he said in a whisper. "Is that the dog that was shot?"

"Yes, his name is Volker. Do you want to pet him?" she asked.

Clarence took a step back away from Volker. "Will he bite me?" he asked in a voice so low we had to lean into him to hear.

"Oh no. He only bites bad people when they are doing bad things. He knows you're helping him by giving him water," she said smiling.

Clarence took a step toward Volker and put out his hand the way Ava showed him. Volker sniffed it and sat down with his tongue hanging out in a big doggie smile.

"See, he's smiling at you," she said.

"Did you ever see him with the two people who owned him, walking him or taking him for a car ride before he was shot?"

"Sometimes. I'd see him with the two people who lived there. They would sit on their front porch with him," he said barely in a whisper. "Are they okay?"

"Well, the lady is in the hospital and she's doing okay," Ava said while Clarence continued to pet Volker.

"I guess the man is dead. I only saw the lady leave in the ambulance with you," the boy said looking at Ava.

"Yes, you're right, and they almost killed Volker. Did you see Volker get shot that day?" Ava asked.

Clarence just nodded with his head down looking at the ground.

"Did you get a good look at the men who went into that house and then came out and shot this dog?" she asked.

"I saw them in the car before they put on the masks," he said so softly, we almost had to read his lips.

Yes! I said to myself in a loud thought.

"Do you know who they are?" Ava asked.

"I do, but my parents don't want me to talk to the police," he said.

"We're not the police," Ava said.

I shook my head 'no' in agreement with Ava.

"We won't tell anybody you told us if you know who they are," Ava said.

"They are really bad men," he said. "That boy you were talking to on the bike. About a year ago they shot his dad. They scare me."

"Well, we won't tell anybody you know who they are," Ava said. "Cross my heart."

"You pinky swear?" Clarence asked.

Ava and I nodded. Then, we each took turns twisting our little fingers together with his to seal the deal in the most sacred—pinky swear ritual.

"They drove back in the red car after you left with the dog," he said.

"We saw the red car. Do you know who it belongs to?"

"No. The next day it pulled into the garage over there," he said, tilting his head to indicate which way up the street. He was careful not to look in that direction.

"Which house?" Ava asked.

Clarence stood looking down and twisting his foot into the grass and said in a whisper, "I'm scared he'll know I told you."

"Who lives in that house?" Ava asked. "Is it just one man?"

"Sometimes there's more than one man. A Spanish lady lives there too. I haven't seen her since the day the dog was shot."

"Do you know her name?"

"No. Maybe she's their sister," Clarence said looking at his foot twisting a small hole in the ground with the toe of his shoe.

"Why do you think that?" Ava asked. "Because they are all Spanish?"

He shrugged and said in all but a whisper, "I guess. They all leave together some mornings and come back together, like a family. The ladies looked alike but didn't dress alike."

By now, Ava and I were bending over to better hear what the boy was saying. He spoke very softly.

"What do you mean they didn't dress alike?" I asked.

"I don't know. My mother said the lady on this side of the street wore short skirts, and she should dress like the lady on the other side of the street."

"When's the last time you saw that lady they give a ride to?" I asked.

"The day the dog got shot. I saw them in the car together when I was on the school bus going down Carrollton. That same day, when I was getting off the school bus, I saw one Spanish lady come back and go into the house on this side of the street. She parked the brown car in that driveway," he said nodding toward the Perez house, "and went into the house on this side of the street."

"Are you sure it wasn't the lady who lives with the dog?" Ava asked.

"Pretty sure. That lady never comes over to this side of the street," Clarence said.

"Did you see the lady leave again that day?" I asked.

"Un huh. I was studying like you just saw me…in the window. She came out, and before she got in the car she prayed by that holy statute," Clarence said as the hole he was twisting the toe of his foot in was getting bigger.

"Which house exactly did she go in?" Ava asked.

"It's the house with the green door," he said without looking in that direction.

Chapter Nineteen

Saturday Afternoon

AVA AND I walked Volker back to my car on Clarence's side of the street, opposite the Perez home. Volker started growling when we got close to the house with the green door. He pulled on his leash and wanted to get to that door in a big way. It took both of us to drag him along across the street to the car. Even in the car he growled with his hair standing up down his back.

"Volker got a whiff of the house with the green door, or he recognized it," Ava said. "He doesn't like it."

"According to one of those kids, the guy you questioned on the day of the shooting," I said to Taylor once we were back in my car, "saw a red Camaro pull into that garage," I said, not giving up Clarence as pinky swear promised.

"Which kid? I need to go back and talk to him," Taylor said.

"We didn't get any names and we don't know where they live," I said. "Think of it as an anonymous tip."

"When you questioned him, did he say a Spanish lady lived with him?" Ava asked.

"No. He said he lived there alone," Taylor said.

Ava and I looked at each other.

Taylor called to get a search warrant based on an anonymous tip. He called for backup in unmarked cars to sit on the house until the warrant got there in case anybody got the idea to leave in the red Camaro. He really didn't know what to do with us and Volker.

"If you get a warrant for the garage and there's a red Camaro in it, can it cover the house too? I mean, if the car is there, then maybe their clothes are still there with Volker's DNA on that hoodie the shooter was wearing," I said.

"I think you're catching on to this police work a little more," Taylor said.

Ava smiled at me.

"I'll go creep around the back and take a peek in that garage," I said.

"Wait," Taylor started to say, but he was distracted by the other end of the call he was on. Too late. I was off walking to the corner with Volker. I figured Volker would alert me to any danger incoming.

At the corner I walked between the last two houses and started working my way to the rear alley that ran behind the houses cutting the block in half. Garbage trucks and the utility companies serviced the residential needs via these alleys. I made my way to the garage that belonged to the house with the green door. Easy enough. He painted the garage door facing the alley green, too. This should be easy enough for the police to find.

I tried to lift the door, but it was either the heaviest door in the world or locked. I peered down both sides of the garage and no side doors. I went over a house and entered their backyard. Hiding behind a wood fence, I could see through the slats that the only door into the garage was facing the back of the house. Great, anyone inside had a clear view of that garage door.

Ava answered her cell phone on the first ring. "What did you find?"

"Nothing yet. The only door to get into that garage is facing the back of his house and there's a glass kitchen door he might see me through. Can you and Taylor go back and keep him at the front door for like two minutes? I'll be quick."

I could hear her telling the plan to Taylor and Taylor demanding that I come back to our vehicle immediately. After what sounded like a lovers' spat, Ava came back on the call and said, "Okay, we'll do it but I'm keeping this line open so you can hear when we leave."

"Genius. Give me a minute to get to the back of his garage again. I'm in the neighbor's yard, next door, behind a fence." As I made my way to the garage, I picked up a stick and moved into position out of sight.

"I'm ready," I said to Ava. "Now, we go radio silent

until we're back in the car or you hear me screaming for help."

"You're a riot," Ava said. "We're walking up to the green door now."

Once I heard the guy who had been so rude to Ava and I answer the door, I started moving. I was walking bent over pulling Volker close to me along the side of the garage. We got to the door facing the back of the house. I could see through the glass door; it was the kitchen. Now, I was out in the open and could easily be seen. I had to get back out before the guy slammed the door on them. I hoped that guy was a little more talkative than he was with Ava and me.

After I was inside, I stayed bent over so no one would see movement through the glass on the top half of the garage door. Using the stick I picked up, I raised the tarp and there was a car, only not a Camaro. It was a Porche 911…silver gray. It also had a vanity plate, but it wasn't the ALL MINE. I took a photo of the plate and where the VIN number should have been also.

I heard muffled voices just outside the garage. I froze, not by intention but by fear. Volker started to growl, a low, throaty growl. I was afraid he would escalate to barking and he had a very loud bark.

Through a window I saw two guys, twenty something, dash by and hurry into the house through the back door. They didn't see me, and I didn't want them to hear Volker. I put my visibly shaking hand over Volker's mouth like a muzzle.

"Shhh, easy boy, good boy. Quiet," I managed to whisper close to his ear while scratching his neck with my other hand. Usually, neck scratching calmed my Meaux. I hoped this was universal dog signal to calm them down. "Quiet Volker, Good boy." I put the tarp back with the stick in one hand holding Volker's muzzle with the other working as fast as I could. I got on the cell and texted Ava, 2 *men-shooters?? – just went in house thru back door.*

My heart was pounding so loud it was hurting my ears. I was afraid they would hear my heart pounding and my breathing, not to mention Volker growling all the way to the front door.

I couldn't take a chance now that there were three people in the house who could look out the back door at the garage and see me leave, duck-walking with a Giant Schnauzer. I unlocked the rear garage door. I lifted it enough for Volker and me to squeeze under so we could get out of there before Volker kicked up a ruckus. I lowered it back down hoping this guy would blame the two that just went into the house for leaving it unlocked.

Back on the street where we had parked, my car was gone. My heart stopped beating thinking they had left me there or had to bug out. Then I saw Taylor moved my car to Nina and Carlos' driveway. Taylor pulled in behind their car. My heartbeat was beginning to return to normal.

I got Volker into the back seat before he started

barking at the green door across the street by distracting him with some dog treats in my pocket.

I showed Taylor the photos I took on my phone and described the two men I saw going in the back door.

"I'll run the plate and VIN. If it's stolen and I'm willing to bet a paycheck it is, I'll call for backup and warrants. We have an anonymous tip that there may be a stolen car in that garage, and now, possibly another stolen car. I bet the two guys who shot Carlos and Nina are in that house," he said.

"I'm not sure it's them," I said.

"Well, someone in that house has something to do with stolen cars if the kid up the block isn't lying."

"Oh, he isn't lying," Ava said and sounded so sure of it, Taylor's head reeled around.

Taylor looked at her and asked, "How can you be sure?"

"He is a gifted kid who does well in school. Why would he lie? The other kids told us he sees everything from his window where he studies," she recovered.

Taylor was in the driver's seat in my car about to start the engine when I said Ava and I had one more thing to do before we could leave.

"Ava, let's go get her mail and see if the neighbor's home. It's almost six o'clock. Nina said he leaves for work at 6:30."

"Wait in the car..." Taylor was trying to tell us as we both jumped out before he could find the auto lock for the doors. "Get back in the car," he said through a two-inch space where he had rolled down his window.

"We'll be right back," I said. Ava just shrugged her shoulders smiling at him.

He lowered the window far enough to hand us two masks and said, "You need to put these on."

We went to Nina's mailbox first and emptied the contents. There were a couple of bills, Entergy and the Sewerage and Water Board among fliers, and junk mail. Next, we walked next door, and I could hear music blasting inside.

It took several knocks on the door before Jason appeared. That gave me time to look through his mail to see if anyone else lived there and get the names. Ava was spinning her hands in the hurry up gesture with her head titled to the door to hear when footsteps approached. Nope, no mail other than Jason Mays.

"Can I help you," a young guy in his twenties, wearing jeans, no shirt, and no shoes answered the door. His dark hair was wet like he just got out of the shower.

"Oh, hi. I hope we didn't interrupt you," I said. "We're friends of Nina and Carlos next door."

He just stood there looking at us. I repeated what I said louder since talking through the mandatory wearing of Covid masks muffled most of what we said.

I plodded on, "We came to get their mail, and I wondered if you took in or accepted any packages for them?"

He leaned his head back away from us saying, "Uh, no. Why would I do that?" Then he looked at his watch.

"To be neighborly," Ava said in her loudest, sweetest, I-can-make-you-fall-in-love-with-me voice. "I'm sorry. I'm Ava and this is Brandy. We told Nina we'd come here and check on her mail."

"Are you two cops?" he asked.

"Oh, no," Ava said while I made a screwed-up face shaking my head in the negative along with her.

"We're friends of Nina's," I added.

He looked at Ava and said, "Sorry, I'm Jason." He extended his hand to shake ours. "No, I haven't taken in any of their mail or packages. Is she…Nina…gonna make it?"

"We're hoping for the best," I said, trying to make it sound as if she might not.

"I heard her husband, and her dog were…" he trailed off.

"Shot. Yes," I said before Ava could answer truthfully that they were very much alive and doing great. I was getting a weird feeling about this guy. It was causing the hair on my arms to stand on end while my skin was starting to tingle. "We're just trying to help her out." I guess he didn't see us parading around the block with Volker for the last thirty minutes.

"I just woke up. I work the night shift, and I was in the shower, getting ready for work when you knocked," he said while looking Ava up and down.

"Do you know why anyone wanted to kill them?" Ava asked.

"No. I mind my own business," he said. "I wasn't even home when it happened."

Ava reached for her neck and touched the chain she was wearing. It was our secret signal we decided on years ago when she could tell someone's lying.

"Nina wanted us to ask you if your girlfriend might pick up the mail for her until she, or we, can come get it?" I asked. It seemed Ava had started to warm him up to us. He was smiling in a way that creeped me out. His eyes were doing the up and down thing on Ava.

"My girlfriend? I don't have a girlfriend. Come in," he said and moved aside to let us enter. "Nina and Carlos were nice people. The woman they are referring to is Spanish, like them. Maybe they knew her from the neighborhood, but I don't know for sure. She paid to rent a room here and that was only for a few days, a week at the most. Are you sure Nina wanted you to ask her?"

"She said the Spanish lady living next door, but she's been heavily sedated. Maybe Nina's confused. Do you know how to get in touch with her? Nina asked us to see if she would keep an eye on her side of the house until she can get home," I said, making this up as I went along since now, he seemed cautiously friendly.

"I lost track of her," he said.

Ava was touching her chain again.

"You might break that chain if you keep pulling on

it," Jason said to Ava.

"Oh, it's a habit, like biting your nails," she said.

"I'll do it for Nina. Like I said, I lost track of Mercedes after she moved across the street. I wasn't even sure they ever met, but if they did, it was probably when I was at work. Like I said, she lived here a short while, and then she moved in with the guy across the street. She had an expensive habit and when she found out he had what she liked, she spent more time over there than here," Jason said.

"Oh, sorry," Ava said touching her neck again.

"It was just a temporary thing," he said. "No big deal."

I looked around his side of the double which was a mirror image of Nina's side. I asked him, "What is Mercedes last name?"

"Gomez or Gutierrez, I think. But I doubt it's her real name. She was a bit of a hustler. She hustled her way into living with me until something better...for her...came along," he said nodding across the street. "I complained when I noticed my watch was missing. She got all self-righteous and left. I know she stole it to buy drugs across the street."

"The young guy? The one sixteen or seventeen years old?" I asked.

"Not sure which one it is. Seems there's always someone going in and out of there. It's the house with the green door," he said.

"We are truly sorry," Ava said. while her hand remained at her neck. "If you'll take in Nina's mail, we'll come back and pick it up for her."

"Sure thing. I'm a bartender in the Quarter so I work every night. I leave here by 6:30 and get home anywhere between 4:00 and 5:00 a.m."

"Wow, that's a long night," I said.

"Here's my card," he said handing it to Ava. "Call me and let me know when you're coming. Next time, I'll have a glass of wine to offer you."

We each smiled a thank you and left. Once we were out of earshot of Jason Mays and before we got into the car Ava said in a low voice, "He's lying about everything."

Once we were back in my car, I said to Taylor, "We just connected a Spanish woman to the drug dealers across the street named Mercedes Gutierrez. Might not be her real name. She could be the Jane Doe you have in the morgue. I have a feeling it might be the same gun that killed Carlos. She used to live with this guy, Jason Mays. He could be involved."

"We questioned this guy a couple of days after the shooting. He said he wasn't home," Taylor said flipping through is leather bound notebook. "He didn't mention a girlfriend or roommate. Said he lived alone. Called his work, but they haven't returned the call."

"I think he gave you a bogus number. Let's see what he gave us," I said. "He says he leaves here at 6:30 in the evening and doesn't get home until 4:00 to 5:00 a.m. Odd thing is restaurants with bars are on a curfew to close by 10:00 p.m. and no bars are open all night."

"The card he gave me, says he works at a bar on

Frenchman Street. I've never heard of it, but that doesn't mean anything since I've been gone so long," Ava said looking at the card.

"That place is only a bar. It's a little hole in the wall. It's small, so if people have to stand six feet apart, one could be the bartender inside and one patron would have to stand outside and yell out his order," I said.

"His card also says LIVE MUSIC NIGHTLY," Ava read. "I'll call this number and see who's playing tonight."

"There's no food served there, and I think all they have for the live music they are touting is one musician squeezed into a corner on weekends."

After Ava listened to a recording she hung up and said, "There's a recording saying the place is closed until further notice, due to the mandated order by the Mayor of New Orleans. Actually, I censored that message for you since whoever made the recording is not a big fan of the Mayor or her lockdown mandate."

"Well, there's no live music in this phase of the lockdown. So, where's he going every day on the same 6:30 schedule if that bar isn't open? If he really is on a schedule like Nina said, and he just confirmed? If so, then he should have been home when they were shot," I added.

"Looks like we need to question him again," Taylor said.

"Yes," Ava said. "He lied to us and he's hiding something."

Chapter Twenty

Saturday

WHEN WE GOT back to my car after talking to Jason Mays, Taylor was sitting in the driver's seat making calls. An unmarked car had pulled up at the end of the next street and radioed Taylor. He drove to meet that car and handed me the keys and asked if I would please take Volker to his house. I said I'd make sure Ava got home safely as she left the back seat with Volker and hopped in the front passenger seat next to me. I moved behind the wheel. He got into the front seat of the unmarked car. Taylor had a clear view up the street to the house with the green door.

Once we were on our way to his house to drop Volker. Ava said, "Jason was lying about the girlfriend and not being home."

"What was a lie?"

"Practically all of it. He said she wasn't his room-mate, but that wasn't true," she said. "She was something more than a roommate but not, technically a girlfriend."

"Maybe she was a more of a business partner or a

friend with benefits?" I asked. "She had to be more than a roommate, because where would she sleep? Does this guy think we're idiots? It's a one bedroom, one bath shotgun, like next door. All he had was two small armchairs in the living room. If she lived there, as a roommate, she would have had to sleep pushing his bean bag chairs together on the floor or, maybe in the kitchen. She could have lined up any chairs to lie across the seats, assuming he has enough for a person to lay down on."

"Good point. He asked us in when we mentioned his girlfriend. We seemed to make him nervous. I think he asked us in to give him time to think of a good excuse as to why she no longer lived there."

"Oh, you're getting good at this," I said. "His place gave off mixed signals."

"Why? He had nice things."

"He did have nice things that only a lot of money can buy, like expensive leather furniture. Jiff has those same armchairs. He has the biggest TV screen I've ever seen."

"It took up the entire wall," Ava said.

"And a wicked bad stereo with speakers almost as tall as you are," I said. "The look was contemporary modern with a bean bag chair chaser. All the trappings of a good drug dealer's success with a hint of where he came from. Remember what Carlos and Nina's place looked like by comparison?"

"Right. It was sparse, but neat and clean."

"The desk looked new and pricey with an Apple computer, the big one, and the latest iPhone sitting on top. Neither are the low end of the product line in price," I said. "He's a bartender, he could make good tips at the right place, but the place on his card? I don't think so. Besides, bartenders and musicians are hardest hit right now with the pandemic. Any bar that doesn't serve food is closed. Even if a place serves food, the mandate is people can't sit at the bar," I said. "So where does he go every day at 6:30?"

"You're right. I remember we were a little early for that appointment. I made it for after work at 5:30. I remember looking at my watch that was in my face when you pushed me down on the seat and it was 5:15. I hope that landlord isn't still waiting," she said laughing. "I gave those times to the police in my statement."

"I did too," I said. "I got back here after the run to the vet at about 6:30. We should have seen him leave, right?"

"And Jason couldn't have been home, or he should have come out to see what was going on. Looks like he's working a long shift somewhere else if that bar isn't open," I said.

"You know, he also mentioned he'd have wine for us there, at his home, when we came back for mail. He didn't invite us to the bar," Ava pondered.

"Because, that bar isn't open," I said a little too loudly. "Do you want to sit in one of his bean bag chairs with a glass of wine? He did have two nice leather armchairs. If we both showed up for wine, I bet he would grab one and park you in the other. That leaves me rolling around the floor trying to sit upright in a bean bag chair trying not to spill my wine."

Ava started to laugh trying to say, "I'm finding that visual hilarious. You forgot he has a desk chair."

"I'm here to keep you entertained. I can't imagine why the roommate left his place to live in the palatial abode cross the street that I can only describe as empty beer bottle style from what I could see of inside over his shoulder the day he slammed the door in our face."

"Well, he didn't update his empty bottle style except to maybe collect more of them," she said.

"So, tell me, how did y'all keep Mr. Green Door talking while I was in the garage. Did Taylor taser him or cuff him?"

"He was a lot different after he saw the badge. He talked to Taylor a whole lot nicer compared to how rude he was with us. Almost like he was a model citizen. Taylor said he was just doing a follow up call to see if he remembered anything from the evening of the shooting. Taylor asked if he lived there alone."

"What did he say?"

"He said he was the only one who lived there. He didn't hear or see anything until he came out for a 'breath of fresh air', which is exactly what he told Taylor the first time he questioned him. He's lying."

"Did y'all hear the two come in the back door or

get to see them?"

"Yes, but they walked through the living room behind Mr. Friendly," she said. "Taylor asked who was that and did they live there? He said that was his sixteen-year-old nephew and a friend. He said it was his dead sister's son. The dad is in jail, so his nephew came around sometimes."

"Well, where does a sixteen-year-old go around other times, I wonder."

"Taylor just tread lightly since we were your cover. He was being nice, trying to keep him there talking so you could get in and out of the garage. He really just reviewed what the guy told him last time," she said.

"Taylor's smooth, I'll give him that. Dante would have gone in like a bulldozer."

"Oh, yeah. But those two guys flew past the front door and went into a room in front of the house, next to the living room and slammed the door. They weren't coming out to talk to anybody," she said. "And that guy just acted as if he didn't see them come in."

"Back to Jason Mays, our bartender—who has no bar to work in but says he pulls all night shifts. I have a hard time believing he couldn't get his hands on the expensive stuff his roommate used."

"That was a lie by omission. Jason said Mercedes could get it across the street," Ava said. "He said he wasn't home when it happened, but there's something else that bothers me with what he said. I can't put my finger on it."

"Why couldn't he get it for her...right across the street?" I said more to myself than in conversation. "Since he was bare-chested when he answered the door, I did notice there were no scratches or dog bite on either arm. But you're right, there's something about him that rubs me the wrong way."

We drove in silence a few minutes, both of us thinking.

"We should follow him," I said.

"What? Are you serious? He'll make us in a heart-beat."

"No, he won't. I have a plan," I said looking at my watch. "We'll go tonight and follow him when he leaves for work."

Chapter Twenty-One

Saturday Afternoon

WHILE I DROVE, Ava called Detective Taylor. When he answered, she put him on speakerphone and asked, "When you questioned the guy living next door to Carlos and Nina, did he say where he was at the time of the shooting?"

"He said he wasn't home. He said he had just left for work, so he didn't hear or see anything, and he wasn't there when we showed up right after the shooting." The sound of Taylor flipping pages in his notebook was all I could hear.

"Are you still there?" I asked.

"Oh yeah, he told us the same thing."

"Was there a car in the driveway?" I asked.

More page flipping. "I don't have a note or license plate...so, no."

"There was no car in his driveway today either. I wonder how he gets to work?" I mused more to myself than to Taylor and Ava.

"He told me he took the streetcar or the bus," Taylor said. "He made the comment that parking in the

French Quarter is difficult and expensive."

"Does he watch the news? There's no one in the French Quarter right now due to the virus," I said. "Parking is wide open and free. Ava and I just talked to him and he said a couple of interesting things. He had a Spanish lady living with him that he claims moved out and into the house with the green door because she had expensive taste for the product the Green Door could provide her," I said.

"What else?"

"He says he goes to work every day and leaves at 6:30 p.m. Well, if that's true, he would have been home when the shooters hit Carlos and Nina's house. Those walls down the middle of that old double are so thin, I bet he could have heard Carlos or Nina change their minds."

There was a pause, and I couldn't even hear him breathing on the other end.

"Taylor, are you still there?"

"Yeah. We need to talk to him again," Taylor said.

"Did he tell you where he worked? Because this card he gave Ava has a number to a tiny bar on Frenchman Street. Think walk-in closet with a beer tap and bar stools. That place should be closed during this phase of the pandemic because it doesn't serve food.

"Also, he said the Spanish lady roomed with him only a few days, but Ava and I think she was a girlfriend or a runner for the drugs or doing something he's involved in. Jason Mays implied she had an expensive habit, and how else do you feed that habit if you're not involved in drugs?"

"You don't unless you're stealing or working the street," he said.

"If she moved across the street to live at the house with the green door like Jason Mays told us, where is she? You could ask your guy who just goes out for a breath of fresh air where did she go." I said. "Didn't you say the body found burned in the East had dental work done out of the country?"

"Yeah, but there are a lot of immigrants and illegals here. Doesn't mean it's her," he said.

"Did autopsy do anything on Carlos in the way of dental?" I asked.

There was a significant pause and I heard him tapping his pen on something.

"I'll call you back," he said hanging up.

We pulled into the driveway at Taylor's house and took Volker out to the yard first before we all settled inside. We sat in his living room going over what we found out. Volker sat in front of Ava on the sofa with his giant head in her lap. She stroked his head, neck and ears while we talked.

Both of us sat quietly mulling over all the information we were told trying to connect the dots. Finally, Ava said, "I can't think without a glass of wine. Want some?"

"Sure. You pour, and I'll recap. Feel free to jump in and add anything I miss or leave out. Here's my theory:

"Jason doesn't add up. – goes to work, promptly every day with no job. Spanish woman (Jane Doe killed/shot with same bullet as Nina and Carlos doesn't add up. I'm thinking if the Spanish Jane Doe has out of the country dental work done the same or similar to Carlos, she can solve this. Note to self, find out if all of Mexico has same dental procedures or processes."

"How are we going to find that out?" Ava asked.

"I thought you had friends in the FBI?"

"Oh right. I could tap one for general info," she said offering her glass to mine in a toast. "Let's solve this so we can get onto the important stuff...your wedding."

Taylor called me and Ava to tell us, "Officers checked with Nina's workplace and found out she hadn't come to work the day she was shot. The dental work done on the burned body of the Spanish woman found matches the same type of work Carlos Perez had. Either they went to the same dentist out of the country, or all Mexican dentists go to the same dental school."

We had him on speakerphone. Ava muted it a second. "Good. I can save my FBI contact for another time," Ava said holding up her glass. Then she unmuted him.

"Have you ever located Nina's cell phone? Or do you have a timeline on her day?" I asked.

"Why, what are you thinking?" Taylor asked and Ava perked up.

"Well, for one thing, if we have Nina, we should

have her cell phone, right? Something is way off on all of this. It's starting to come together for me. It's just not there yet. Can we call you back? I need to work through a couple of scenarios," I said.

"Yes, but call me and not the Captain, please."

"Of course. I want you indebted to me when you get that big promotion from solving this case based on my theory. You will remember it was me who shared the information with you," I said. "If you don't, I'll remind you. Wait. Did you find Carlos's cell phone at the scene?"

"Yeah, we did. Why?"

"Any texts or messages from Nina to Carlos?" I asked.

"The IT forensic guys said there were no texts or messages on his phone."

"None, as in zero, not even one?" I asked.

"That's what they said."

"Isn't that strange in this day and age with cell phones and messaging that there's no texts or messages from his wife?" I asked.

"Can't they go back and pull up everything that's ever been deleted?" Ava asked.

"I'll see. Before you ask, we are requesting Nina's phone records from the cell phone provider. She told us she thinks she left it at work."

"Okay, I've got to think," I said. "Bye."

We both sat still in Taylor's living room pondering all the things we thought we knew and what we didn't know.

"So, Ava, here's what I'm wondering. Why does Nina, who kept a nice, loving home from everything I observed that made them the happy couple I saw in photos, never refer to 'our' life, 'our' home, 'our' dog, or 'our' car? Every time she spoke about their life, she said Carlos's dog or Carlos's car. She drove the car. And why does she want to get rid of that beautiful animal that risked his life to save hers?"

We sat for a few minutes thinking.

"Well, some of what Nina said was borderline lying. It's as if she knew the right answers but they weren't her answers," Ava said. "I've never questioned someone who had been so recently traumatized."

"See, that's it. When I went into their side of the shotgun, I got a different story about the couple than what Nina is conveying now. The Nina we met doesn't even feel like the Nina who lived there in the photos with Carlos," I said.

"Like what?"

"Like consistently making comments to get rid of the dog. There were a couple of photos of her and Volker. She was walking him, giving him a treat and in one, she had her arms around his neck. They both looked like they were smiling. She said she can't handle the dog, but in the photos she was. Why does she want to get rid of that dog? Someone is caring for him, and when I told her rescue would pay all the vet bills, she said, she wanted to sell him on Craigslist," I said.

"When did she say that?"

"She called me one day when she couldn't get in touch with you. I can't even remember why she called…oh, right. She said she found a friend from work to stay with. She said she couldn't ask them if she could bring Volker and she couldn't handle him. Carlos did all that."

Ava sat with her chin in her hand, elbow resting on the arm of the oversized leather sofa Taylor had in his living room.

"Plus, Nina hasn't really asked too much about Carlos or asked to see his body, or when she can make funeral arrangements."

"I thought that was odd too. It's like she's moved on already," Ava said.

"So, if the Nina we know isn't the Nina married to Carlos, where is Nina and how did Nina's car and purse get home?" I mused out loud.

Ava said, "Odd thing, I saw Nina's purse and her I.D., but no cell phone, spilled all over the floor the day of the crime."

"Ava, call your buddy back and ask if they searched the Perez car. If they didn't, suggest they do it as soon as possible before Nina gets out of the hospital and gets to it."

"Okay, what are you thinking?"

"I'm thinking that there's something in that car or house that belongs to the real Nina that can prove our Faux Nina is an imposter. Just ask Taylor if they ran

DNA on Nina from a brush or in the hospital, anything that compares the woman in the hospital with the things that belong to her in that house."

She was about to call Taylor when her phone rang. It was Taylor. He told her the search of the house with the Green Door uncovered a stolen car in the garage, but not a red Camaro. Ava asked him about Nina's DNA and if Homicide was sure she was, in fact, the correct Nina Perez.

"We found an empty purse in the trunk of their car," he said. "I'll get it run for fingerprints and DNA. The contents however that spilled out of that purse inside belonged to Nina and had her fingerprints on everything. I'll see if they were on the purse itself. I see where you're going with this."

"Did you ping Nina's phone to see where it is?" I asked.

"Well, the last location we could get from the cell provider was…"

"New Orleans East where the burned body was found?" I asked.

"How do you know that?" Taylor sounded exasperated.

"Because we've been misled since the beginning of this. The only one now I trust is Volker. We must find that hoodie to see if Volker's DNA is on it or if the fibers pulled from his teeth match it." I said.

"Taylor," Ava added, "make sure Nina doesn't leave that hospital yet. We think she'll go for the Perez car and leave town."

"You need to post someone at the Perez home and get them to look under the Madonna statue in the front yard," I added.

"Well, we could do a line-up and see which person Volker wants to rip apart," Taylor said.

"That's a great idea," I said.

"I'm joking. That will never stand up in court…but…that gives me an idea. It might be enough to flush out one of them to make a deal and give up the other," he said.

"OK, we'll talk to you later," I said. I turned to Ava and said, "I have a better idea."

Chapter Twenty-Two

Saturday evening

"WHAT DO YOU have in that crazy mind of yours?" Ava asked.

It was almost 5:30 p.m.

"Well, we have time to do this tonight if we hurry, but we have to use your leased car. C'mon, I'll tell you on the way."

We got Volker settled in the kitchen and put up the gates Taylor had made for the doorways so he couldn't wander throughout the house. We fed him and left.

On the way to Ava's, she asked me, "I don't mind using my car, but why?"

"Because we're going to follow Jason Mays tonight. I want to know what he does all night when there's a citywide, no…statewide curfew in place and the bar he claims to work at is closed. The stolen car across the street in the garage makes me think he's boosting cars, expensive cars, and selling them to those who have the cash to pay for them. Nice cars are constantly being stolen where I live and in the Lakeview area close by."

"This sounds dangerous."

"Yeah, it probably is, but you said Jason is lying about everything. That makes him our numero uno suspect. Too bad he didn't have bite marks on his arms when we saw him…shirtless," I said. "That would have made this way too easy."

"Could mean he was the driver and not the shooter," Ava said.

"Exactly. We just must find that Camaro if we can. It would wrap this up and then I can get married and go on a honeymoon feeling like I've done something to help that brave dog and his late owner, Carlos."

"Well, we officially start the countdown to your big day," Ava said. "It's next Saturday…less than one week. Getting excited?"

"I'm more than excited about our wedding, but I need to put this behind me or Jiff will kill me if I want to postpone our wedding because we haven't found the killer."

I STOPPED AT my apartment and ran in to get a few things. Ava waited in the car. Then, we made our way to Ava's to swap out cars.

"If we follow Jason, won't he recognize us?" Ava asked.

"Look in the bag," I said as I handed her a tote bag full of stuff.

Ava pulled out two wigs, one was a platinum pageboy cut and the other was a dark brown, shoulder length, layered hairstyle much like the one made famous by Farrah Fawcett. Next, she pulled out two extra-large black T-shirts.

"The page-boy is the one I prefer. It flatters my face. I wore it when I was an angel in the Christmas parade."

"You. An Angel?" Ava asked in mock disbelief.

"Of course. Try on the other one and let's see how it looks on you," I said as we pulled into the Towers Parking. "Let's run into the bathroom in the lobby and put these on. I also brought two of Jiff's big T-shirts to cover our clothes. Jason might remember our stylish duds from today since he looked you up and down."

In the lobby ladies' room, we fussed with our hair to get it to stay up under the wigs.

"Where do you get this stuff?" Ava asked.

"Uh…New Orleans gives us one reason after another to wear a costume. I wore this one in the Santa parade, and the one you are going to put on was part of my costume one year in the Easter parade. I also wore it with a big hat I got stuck wearing in a wedding once, but this venue didn't call for the hat."

"Thanks…I guess," she said.

"Besides Mardi Gras there are other fun parades like the Boo parade, the Christmas parade, the Easter parade and the occasional Super Bowl parade here. Everyone has costumes and wigs. You can borrow any of mine until you get some of your own," I said. "We have to leave now, or we might miss him."

"I look like…the Happy Hooker," she said, checking herself out in the mirror on the visor.

"You do not. The hair color will throw him off or anyone else who sees us. We both look drastically different in these. Here, wear some really red lipstick like you normally would NOT wear. I'll wear it too. We must get moving. It's almost 6:30 when he leaves."

We drove to Jason's house and stopped up the street right as he walked out his door heading to the streetcar stop. I grabbed my birdwatching binoculars so we could keep an eye on the streetcar stops to see when he exited.

It was a slow-moving stakeout. I drove Ava's car because I knew the streets and could turn off Carrollton and then fall back in following the streetcar between stops. Jason rode it all the way to the end where it stopped on Canal. He transferred to the Canal line changing again to the Rampart Street line. He got off at Louis Armstrong Park and walked away from the river, down Ursulines Avenue to St. Claude.

By now he was easier to follow until he turned on St. Claude and crossed Esplanade Avenue. I caught a light and he disappeared around a corner. There were lots of businesses and houses intermingled here and if he went inside one, we could lose him. As soon as I got the green light I sped through the intersection and turned at the same corner he did. I was going so fast I almost hit him when he walked out into the street in front of me and looked at the two of us straight in the face.

I held up my hands in apology looking down to avoid eye contact. It had gotten dark by now and I didn't have my sunglasses on. Neither did Ava. Then, I quickly drove around him watching in the rearview mirror to see if he recognized us. He was going about his business getting something out of a car parked on the street.

We drove around the block and came at the corner from another direction so we could park and watch the driveway to see when anyone came along or left. He paid no attention to us or the car. We saw him get a bag from the car parked on the street and walk back down the driveway that led to a sizeable garage at the rear behind what looked like a vacant house. We could see the industrial size garage's roof but not the front of the building.

There was a small restaurant with a bar and food neon sign in the window at on the corner and Ava offered to get us a drink.

"Are you sure you want to go in there?" I asked.

"Yes, and I'll get the license plate on that car Jason just took something out of. I'll casually walk past it," she said.

"Okay, but don't stop. Someone might see you."

"It's dark now. Who's going to see me and if they do, they won't be able to describe me once I take off this wig."

"Keep your cell phone on and in your hand. Mute the ringer. I'm calling you now."

Ava walked down one side of the street away from me and when she got to the corner, she went into the restaurant and came out with what looked like a wine bottle in a paper bag. She held two plastic cups in her other hand.

She looked around as if lost. She walked back down the side of the street where the car Jason took something out of was parked. Just as she got closer, I saw him before she did. He was heading back to the car and the two were on a collision course about to smash into each other if she didn't stop.

"Hide! Hide! Hide!" I screamed into the phone.

She dove behind a big Ligustrum bush in front of a house two doors down from Jason just as he got inside the vehicle and moved it into the driveway. He pulled it all the way down the driveway, stopping up against the extra wide commercial sized garage door facing the street. It was wide enough for three cars to drive into and park next to each other. Jason got out and went back into the garage through a doorway I couldn't see from where we were parked.

"Clear," I said into the phone.

Now, Ava started crawling on hands and knees across two lawns to get a look at the license plate. She looked like an old wino using one hand to hold the paper bag with the wine bottle and crawling with the other hand. Why didn't she just leave the wine and cups under the Ligustrum and go back for them, I wondered.

"He's going to see you. Don't get caught," I was yelling into the phone. I don't know if she could hear me because her phone was not in either hand. When she got into position behind another shrub next door to the end of the driveway, I could see her take her cell phone out from the front of her shirt. She took a photo with her phone and crawled back to her Ligustrum bush. Once she was back in hiding, she sent me the photo she took. A few minutes later she crawled out casually and stood up as if she just walked out of her front door.

Back in the car she asked me if I had a corkscrew in my purse.

"A corkscrew? No. I have one in my car's glove box, why? Did they only serve wine with a cork, in that dump?"

"No, I requested a bottle with a cork and asked them to open it in front of me," she said. "I made a good call since you didn't have one." She poured us each a plastic cup full.

"Before I drink this, I need to see what's in that garage back there," I said.

"Aren't you tired of crawling around in garages and all over the ground? I know I am. Let's call Taylor."

"No, give me a minute to see what's going on back there," I said getting out.

"I'll wait here and call Taylor if you don't come back," she said taking a sip. "You've got two minutes. Cell phone protocol."

Using the same cell phone monitoring skills, we had perfected, for Operation Green Door, I moved in the shadows down the driveway stopping at the side of the house. I waited right there in the protection of the shadows while I decided how to proceed. Good thing I hesitated because the streetlamp in front of the building came on lighting up the entire driveway and side of the house I was leaning against.

Great, of all the streetlights out in the city, this must be the only one that works. I could hear voices coming from the garage. There was a big garbage can at the corner of the building I'd have to step around to get to the window of the garage. I would be seen in the spotlight of that blasted streetlamp.

Before I could make up my mind, I heard a door squeak open and Jason's voice calling out, "I'll be back in a minute. Hold your horses. I've got to put the trash out to the curb."

Footsteps were coming my way. With my luck he would see me the second he rounded the side of the house to go down the driveway. No time to run back to the car. I was about to be found out. I heard the voice inside yell again for him to come back and help with something.

Then, the footsteps stopped. I heard the garbage can scraping as someone opened the lid. The next noise sounded like something metal getting tossed on top of glass. Then the footsteps headed back to the door and Jason was yelling, "I'm coming."

I REACHED AROUND the corner of the building and carefully lifted the garbage can lid. There were five or six car license plates laying on top of a boatload of beer bottles. The plate on top was none other than the ALL MINE vanity plate along with three others.

The fear from a moment ago was gone. I bravely, or foolishly, depends on how you look at it, moved to a window on the garage between my corner hiding place and a door I'm sure Jason entered.

Pressing against the building next to the window, from the angle I was at, I could see the rear of a red Camaro. Now, it had an out of state plate, a Mississippi one, that probably belonged to a car that hadn't noticed it was missing yet.

There was another car, a black BMW next to the Camaro, but I couldn't see more than the logo on the trunk. This was enough. I made my way back along the shadows of the house to the car.

"You were starting to worry me when I didn't have you in my line of vision," Ava said.

"They're changing plates on stolen cars back in that garage. We need to tell Taylor. The Camaro is in there and the ALL MINE license plate is in the garbage can ready to be put out on the curb for pick-up."

Ava called Taylor and relayed the news about the Camaro and the license plates. She gave him the address. After a couple of uh-huhs, she told him we'd wait in place on the stakeout until he got here in case someone left or moved a vehicle.

"Pour me some of that vintage now," I said holding out my plastic cup after Ava hung up. "What is the date? Bottled today? Early this morning?"

TAYLOR ARRIVED WITH another police car; sirens silent, parking opposite us across the intersection at the corner. He looked right at us without a sign of recognition.

Another vehicle arrived on the street coming from the opposite direction. A six-man Tactical Unit got out of a black SUV that stopped halfway down the block from our corner. We watched them move stealthily toward the driveway and suddenly, the streetlight went out. I had to admit, they were a lot better at this than I was and had connections to control Entergy. Impressive.

They were all in place for the raid. I saw Taylor talking on his two-way radio and one of the Tactical guys in the lead was nodding and holding up his hand in a fist to hold position. Then Taylor picked up his cell.

My cell phone rang, and it was him.

"Where are you two? We're about to go in at the location you gave us, and it would be better if you two were outta here."

"We're in Ava's leased vehicle. It's the black Lexus on the corner," I said and paused as he made eye contact with me. "You're looking right at us."

"Where? I see two women in that vehicle drinking

something. It doesn't look like you two, but if it is, I hope it isn't alcohol because you need to leave immediately," he said walking in our direction while he still had his cell phone to his ear.

When he got to our car, I lowered the window. "What the… What are you two doing?"

"It's so no one will recognize us. You didn't," Ava said ever so sweetly.

"One of these days, Alexander, someone is going to call in a stalking or Peeping Tom complaint on you," he said.

"Do me a favor, call or text when you pull them out of that garage. I have a feeling you're gonna find the guys from the house with the green door along with Jason Mays. You can thank us later, we're leaving," I said putting the car in gear and leaving him there looking at our taillights as we drove away.

Chapter Twenty-Three

Saturday night – Tuesday

BACK AT AVA'S, we stayed long enough to pick up my car. We headed to my house to wait for Jiff and feed our dogs.

With wine glasses and a fresh pour in hand, and sitting in our living room with no view, I laid out to Ava my theory of what happened based on known facts. I couldn't wait for Taylor to call and confirm some of my deductions. Jiff would be home by then, and we could tell him the correct version if mine was wrong. I didn't think it would be.

After I told Ava my suspicions, we sat drinking our wine and waiting for Taylor to call.

"Sorry for the lack of a great view here," I said. "We do have entertainment in the way of our Schnauzers."

"If I had to choose, I'd pick a dog over a view," Ava said. "They are just too much fun, and so happy to see us."

"Right answer," I said.

It was an hour later, and Jiff was walking in the front door when Ava's phone rang. "I'm putting you on speakerphone," she told him.

"Yeah, that's fine. I felt, as much as I hate to admit it, I needed to call and thank Alexander. You were right. The crew in that garage was the man from across street in the house with the green door along with his nephew and a friend. Jason Mays was in there, but you knew that. The red Camaro was there. We found the vanity plate along with four others in that garbage can. A hoodie with tears on the sleeve was in the trunk of the Camaro. I'm sure it will match Volker's DNA. The nephew had wounds on his left forearm that still were healing. You said the dog grabbed his left forearm, right?"

"Yes. He shot Volker with his right hand holding the gun," I said.

"I GOT FORENSICS to call the hospital to get DNA on the faux Nina in there and you were right again. The body found shot and burned in the East is Nina Perez. We think the woman in the hospital is the woman calling herself Mercedes Gutierrez according to the nephew. He's wanting a deal and spilling it. We found women's clothes at Jason Mays and across the street. We think they will match her."

"What about the statute?" Ava asked. "Did you find anything there?"

"Oh, and we did find a brick of heroin buried under that statue. It's a match to the woman's fingerprints found on the purse in the Perez house, the one with the contents all over the floor," he said. "How did you know about the heroin?"

"I pieced it together from the kids we talked to," I said. "They saw Mercedes ride to work that morning with Nina. I figured after they dropped Carlos at the store, she makes Nina drive to a remote location, shoots her and takes her purse. Before she tosses Nina's cell phone out there, somewhere in the swamp, she sent a text to her husband, Carlos, saying she was going somewhere after work. From Nina's phone, she texts him saying Mercedes will pick him up like usual and take him home. Mercedes needed time to return the gun to the house with the green door so, when found, the bullets would match tying it to previous crimes. And, it would have worked if she hadn't stolen the drugs."

Jiff sat there shaking his head "My, you've been busy today."

"You're right so far. The IT guys found texts similar to what you just said between Nina and Carlos before her phone stopped working," Taylor said. "There's a lot of swamps out that way. She likely tossed Nina's cell out there."

"So, why is the heroin under the statute?" Jiff asked.

"After Mercedes killed Nina, she returned the gun back to the Green Door, took a brick of heroin and planted it under the Madonna across the street so she can sneak out later that night, boost Carlos's car and retrieve the heroin. This is when a boy getting off the school bus saw the Spanish lady praying at the statue. I think Mercedes planned to take Nina's identification and leave town. Nina would have been a missing person and since car thefts are common in that neighborhood… well…all neighborhoods in the city, it's unlikely anyone would look for that vehicle. With Carlos dead, and getting herself shot, her plan was delayed until she could leave the hospital and go back to their house as Nina Perez."

"We think her plan derailed when Jason and the nephew, realized the heroin was gone and decided to get it back," Ava said.

"Right," Taylor said. "We're finding out a lot from the nephew, but we're trying to get Jason Mays to talk. He's not the shooter so he could get a better deal if he testifies against the others. He'll still do time."

"After the time we spent around the faux Nina, I don't think Mercedes ever thought they'd realize the drugs were gone in time to stop her from leaving with it. I'm sure they were surprised to find her with Carlos," I said.

"Jason Mays said Mercedes moved drugs on the school campus and they used her as a driver from time to time. When the guys across the street told Jason a brick of heroin was missing, he knew it was her and thought she hid it at Carlos and Nina's house since she's been chummy with them, getting rides to work and some temp jobs. So, the nephew and Mays hatched a plan to go in shooting. They figured they would get Carlos to tell them where the drugs were by threatening his wife. Only the wife wasn't there. Mercedes was," Taylor said. "When they realized it was her, they started to shoot her to get her to talk.

"Since we found all of them in the same place with the Camaro that was used in the crime, we searched their homes and found a woman's clothes that we're sure will be a match to Mercedes' DNA. She's been handcuffed to her bed at University Medical Center in the ward they use for prisoners needing medical attention from Parish Prison.

"Once we impounded the Perez vehicle it was discovered the purse found inside the house belonged to Mercedes. The DNA on the purse in the Perez trunk matched the burned body found in the East.

"So, Mercedes was going to take Nina's identification," I said. "What about the gun? Where was it?"

"We found a gun that matches the caliber used to kill both Carlos and Nina Perez at the house with the green door. All the bullets removed from Mercedes Gutierrez, Carlos and Nina Perez matched the weapon found," Taylor said. "The police found it hidden in the bathroom ceiling behind a false vent in the house. According to Jason Mays, that hoodie belongs to the nephew."

"I guess you have enough to charge all of them?" Jiff asked.

"Oh yes," Taylor said. "The nephew spilled on

Jason selling drugs for him and thought Jason sent over Mercedes to steal a brick. Jason said he didn't know she stole the drugs, but she did steal money and a watch from him, so they decided to get the drugs back. Jason ran to the driver's side of car. The nephew was trying to get in on the passenger side, like you said, when the dog attacked him. Only the nephew has marks on his arm that look like a dog bite. Those fibers from the hoodie are also being sent to the lab to see if they match the ones taken from Volker's teeth. I think they will nail the nephew as the shooter between the GSR and the DNA."

"Jason was the first to flip since he didn't shoot anyone. He didn't seem to know that a murder that happens during a crime, ups the charge to felony murder. The uncle is being charged with accessory after the fact."

"I guess I can now start to look for a good home for Volker since he won't be needed at a trial," I said.

"Oh…well…I don't mind fostering him awhile longer," Taylor said.

"You've been really great taking care of him during his recovery and your place is great for a dog his size, but you work long hours and it's not fair for him to be left alone so much. This breed is very social," I said.

"Tell her," Ava said. "He's really stepped up being a foster. Travis just might have raised the bar for future foster homes!"

Ava's now calling him Travis, not Detective Taylor? I

thought.

"Tell me what?" I asked.

"Ava has been helping when I'm working a long day. She has stopped by to walk him, but I found a place to take him for playdates twice a week on Tchoupitoulas Street, a Camp BowWow. I signed him up there, and I found a dog walker to come take him out every day at noon for an hour's walk or to the dog park. I subscribed to a membership there also," Taylor said.

"You are what we in rescue call a Foster Failure," I said. "I guess this means you want to adopt him?"

"Well…yeah," Taylor said. "I really don't work nearly as much as I did in New York and it's nice to have a smiling face waiting on the other side of the door for me when I get home."

TUESDAY, BEFORE MY wedding, Taylor called, and Ava put him on speakerphone. He confirmed Volker's DNA and the nephew's DNA were on the sweatshirt. They had their guy.

Taylor found multiple warrants open for the nephew who lived with the uncle at the house with the green door including grand theft auto, distributing substances to minors and unlawful use of a weapon. Now, murder was added to the list. The nephew's prints and Mercedes' prints were found on the gun.

Mercedes confessed to telling the nephew that Carlos and Nina had money because they were helping people get to New Orleans. She assumed they were illegally buying transit for their relatives. She told the nephew she planned to rob them, but when she realized they didn't have that kind of money she wanted, she decided to rob the drug dealers and leave in the Perez car. She hatched a plan that would give her a couple of hours lead time to get out of town with the drugs.

Taylor added before he hung up that he really wished he knew who to thank for the anonymous tip that busted the car theft ring on St. Claude Avenue.

Chapter Twenty-Four

Wednesday

AVA SAW A notice in the paper for a memorial that was being held at the community college on Wednesday afternoon for Nina Perez outside under the trees. She and I decided to go even though we never met her. About six people showed up along with Ava and me. We all wore masks and maintained social distance.

I felt like I knew Nina from what we saw in her home and from the dog who loved them enough to risk his life trying to save them. We learned Nina had a stellar work and school record from her peers who attended the ceremony. After the service, two teachers, wearing masks and staying the recommended social distance, hung around to support each other over the loss of their colleague.

One teacher came closer to us and we introduced ourselves. This lady told us, "Nina got Mercedes a part time job working as casual labor, or on call as needed, at the college. I managed that schedule, and she wasn't scheduled or called into work that day. We found it odd when Nina never showed up for work or school. She never missed a day. I was going to call the police if she didn't show up the next day, but then I heard on the news there was the homicide at their address."

"Did you read where the woman shot was presumed to be Nina Perez in the hospital?" Ava asked.

"Yes, we did think it was Nina. They withheld her name, but I recognized her address because I would sometimes give her and Carlos a ride before and after work when they had car trouble. They didn't live very far from me. Two of us went to the hospital to visit her, but we were told she didn't want any visitors. We left without seeing her and thought that was very odd, but then, we figured she was dealing with the loss of her husband along with being shot."

This teacher called another over saying she was the one who went with her to the hospital and got turned away.

The second teacher said, "If we had seen her, we would have known right away it was Mercedes. I told Nina not to trust her. I'd find things missing from my classroom when she had been there to clean. Nothing expensive. A crystal desk clock a student had given me and my raincoat I left in the cloak room one night went missing on a day she worked in my classroom. Nina said she needed help. Nina made excuses for her, and had said she was in a bad situation, but trying to turn her life around."

"She even invited her home one evening for a

meal," the first teacher said. "Nina had a big heart. She said they all talked about missing their relatives still in Mexico. Nina and Carlos told her they were working on getting all their family here. I worried something like this would happen if Mercedes thought they had money hidden someplace. She had an obvious drug problem, but Nina refused to accept it. Nina once said that Mercedes was like her sister back home and she hoped someone would help her sister like she tried to help Mercedes. Carlos tried to tell Nina what she was like, but Nina wouldn't listen. I really think she stayed chummy with Nina to figure out how rob them."

I said, "Thank you for having this for Nina. We didn't know her, but we were there when they shot her husband and Mercedes. We tried to help figure out who did it."

When Ava spoke to Taylor again, which is hourly now, or so it seems. She relayed what we learned from the teachers.

"Don't worry, we have plenty of time to figure out who she really is, but not because she'll get out anytime soon. She shot and killed Nina Perez and was responsible for the death of Carlos Perez in a drug related crime. She'll be a guest of the state for a long time," Taylor said.

Chapter Twenty-Five

Friday

IT WAS FRIDAY, the day before my wedding, and I took the day off from work to finalize any last-minute preparations. Everything I had planned for the initial wedding date had been documented by the Heinkel's event planner and was being carried out for tomorrow with the minor adjustment of guests attending.

I had nothing to do except show up at this point. I did have to pick up our rings and my wedding gift to Jiff. So, I took this time to go to the jewelers in Canal Place for the rings. We were having tomorrow's date engraved inside the bands. No changing the date this time without getting new bands.

I stopped in Saks to pick up a leather-bound, desk planner and calendar as my wedding gift to Jiff. It was something he would look at every day. Saks offered to engrave his initials in gold. They said it would take an hour or so. I wrote in the planner our wedding date one year from tomorrow and put a kiss on that page for our one-year anniversary. Saks even wrapped it for me, so I had nothing to do but wait for tomorrow to begin.

Jiff had said to plan to take a couple of days off so we could head to a beach for a short, but private honeymoon. He said he had a surprise for me so pack a weekend bag of fun, cool clothes and a swimsuit. I assumed we were going to the family's condo in Florida.

Feeling a little overwhelmed at not having much time to better prepare for what I should bring with me, I called Ava to meet me at Canal Place to do shopping for a last-minute trousseau. She had to finish up a few things and said she'd make it over by three o'clock at the latest.

To KILL SOME time while I waited for Ava and Saks to wrap Jiff's gift, I browsed around Saks and found a swimsuit and a great sundress on sale. There was a new pair of strappy sandals I had just bought for the summer and hadn't worn yet, so this new dress would be perfect with them for a dinner or shopping.

There were a couple of ladies' fashion stores in the mall, so I took the time to wander through them. I found a great pair of shorts, a couple of T-shirts and a swim cover-up at one store. I wanted something extra pretty and special in the way of lingerie, so I called Ava and said I was heading over to the Trashy Diva on Royal Street and asked her to meet me there.

"I'm almost at Canal Place," she said.

"Okay, I'll meet you at the back entrance and we

can walk there together," I said. "You will like this store and you will want to come back. It's a ladies clothing store that had a crazy terrific line of one-of-a-kind, timeless apparel inspired by classic, vintage trends."

"A new job, new place hasn't really left time for me to check out the shopping here," she said.

"Their clothes flatter all body-types, and they are all sexy. Trashy Diva specializes in accessories, clothing and lingerie. They even have great, vintage inspired high heel shoes."

We were still chatting when she met me. We walked over to Royal Street together. I found a honeymoon-worthy nightgown I could not resist for our trip. I realized I hadn't gotten anything pretty or sexy to wear under my wedding dress, so I found a white, strapless bustier with garters, white lace panties and some silk stockings, not pantyhose. Now, I was ready.

It was almost five o'clock when Jiff called asking me how my day was going. I told him Ava and I were heading to Canal Place to have a glass of wine in the Westin bar as soon as I picked up something that was ready at Saks. He was welcome to join us. He said he had to finish up a few things so he wouldn't be called on our honeymoon, and he'd see me at home later. He told me to have fun with Ava.

AVA WAS ALREADY taking in the magnificent view in the lobby from the oversized, comfy chairs when I joined her with my gift from Sak's.

"The view here is fantastic like the one in Jiff's condo of Lake Pontchartrain. You can see it from every window. You two should move there. I'm spoiled with great views and I don't think I'll find an apartment with a view like this or one of the lake."

"You never know," I said.

A waiter appeared with two glasses of wine and placed them on the table in front of us. We toasted and took a sip.

"You don't need a house with a yard, do you?" I asked.

"No, not really," she said.

"What about the high-rise apartments in the River-bend area of Uptown? They are nice, have great views and your dad is halfway between there and work. It's a professional crowd that lives there. It's not far from where…" I paused for effect, "Travis lives."

Ava acted like she didn't hear me. "Let's go look there after your wedding weekend…"

"Sounds like the perfect plan," I said.

"You got some beautiful sexy things for your trip and wedding. I loved that store. I will be going back there to shop. You are set. Any idea where you're going?"

"No, and while I'm a big planner, it's nice to have someone else think of all the details. I feel like the Princess in the Royal Wedding."

"I'm glad for you. We should all be a Princess on

our wedding day!"

We toasted our glasses to Nina and Carlos, and again, to my wedding the next day. We finished our drinks and I drove Ava to her car back at our building and went home to meet Jiff.

"TOMORROW IS FINALLY here," Jiff said when he strolled in early from work at 6:30 p.m. "Let's go get a drink and dinner somewhere and relax tonight. My mother said everything is ready at home."

"Shouldn't we go over there to see if we can help?" I asked wringing my hands.

"No," he said taking my hands and holding one of mine in each of his. "My mother said to take the evening and relax so we're not stressed tomorrow. I'm sending the car to pick up your parents first, then Felix will come here to get you. I'm going to stay at my parents' house tonight after we have dinner together."

"Let's go to the Elysian Patio Bar in Hotel Peter and Paul," I said. "We can sit out there, relax and have dinner and a drink. Remember, we thought about having our ceremony there, but they were all booked."

"Yes, that is a great place," he said kissing each hand.

ONCE WE WERE seated at a table, Jiff said, "I'll get up early under the pretense of helping my mother. I really don't need to because she will make sure everything is perfect. She loves a party, and she has that event planner trained."

"I'll arrange a car to take my parents home after the ceremony," I said.

"No need. Felix will be waiting to take them home or we'll send them in the backup limo."

"Wait. What? Y'all have a backup limo?" I asked.

"Yes, because there's so many of us always moving around," he said smiling.

"Well, that is really nice, but I can rent a limo, and have it pick me up and then stop to get my parents," I said.

"Why? I'm not letting you rent a limo when we have the two cars at our disposal. We have access to it 24/7, so we might as well use it. I already have Felix picking me up later tonight, so you can spend tomorrow doing all the stuff you want to do before our ceremony," he said. "Felix will pick you up and take your luggage for our weekend also. So, pack before he gets there. Besides, with Felix's experience in the martial arts, I kinda like having him escort you places. It's a wicked world we live in."

"Jeffrey is doing my hair and makeup for the ceremony, so that will take time," I said. "After she finishes, Felix can pick me up first and then pick up my parents. I don't want to expose him to my mother without me there running interference."

"Sounds like a plan," he said kissing my hand.

Jeffrey met me at my apartment at 10:00 a.m. Ava arrived a few minutes before her with a box of croissants from Croissant d'Or. Suzanne was already home and joined us while I had my hair and makeup done. Jeffrey brought a bottle of Moet Chandon to start the day off.

"Y'all are the best," I said.

"This will also help you better cope with your mother'," Jeffrey said.

"This is the perfect wedding day breakfast," Ava said. "Croissants and Champagne! I want this when I get married."

I arranged to have lunch delivered after my hair, makeup, and nails were done, even though I couldn't eat a bite after the croissants and champagne. Ava and Suzanne insisted I eat something so a glass or two of champagne after the ceremony would not go straight to my head.

"There's nothing worse than a tipsy bride," Suzanne said.

As scheduled, Felix arrived in Mr. Heinkel's Rolls Royce promptly at 3:30 for me. Arriving at the same time was the stretch limo Jiff sent to take Suzanne and Ava to his parents' home ahead of me.

When I got into the back seat, I got so nervous my hands were visibly shaking. I had to get it together on the way uptown to pick up my parents. I'm sure my dad would have a million questions. I directed Felix as to how he could make the shortest drive to the Heinkel home with my mother in the car.

With every block closer to my parents' home, I

started to shake even more. I should have gone in the stretch with Ava and Suzanne. I should have sent my mother, alone, in the stretch. I should have taken a tranquilizer. I should have taken the streetcar. I should take a breath.

After doing several deep breathes on a four count in, and a four count out, I started to regain my composure. Good. We just pulled up to my parents' home.

Felix was right on schedule. My dad came out wearing a tuxedo, and as he got in, I said, "You look dashing. I hope Jiff can measure up."

He kissed me on the cheek, and he teared up. He just nodded and sat across from me.

My mother, on the other hand, said, "A Rolls? Really Brandy. You really know how to waste money."

"This is the Heinkel's car and driver. They sent it to pick us up as a courtesy." And just like that, my hands stopped shaking.

My dad gave her a look I'd never seen before. She remained quiet for the rest of the ride.

At the guard gate, a uniformed guard waived us through. My mother was about to open the car door when we pulled up and stopped in front of the Heinkel's home. I put my hand on hers to stop her and left it there until Felix got out and opened our door, offering my mother his hand to assist her. Once she was out of the car, he offered his hand to me.

As we made our way up to the front door, I noticed

the look of shock on my mother's face which could have reflected what mine might have looked like the first time I visited the Heinkel home. Grand didn't begin to describe it and it was quite intimidating.

My dad said to her as we walked up the front marble stairs, "I don't know why you didn't get a new dress for Brandy's wedding." I could have kissed him.

The Heinkel's butler greeted us at the front door. He asked my mother politely, to wait a moment while he announced our arrival to Mr. and Mrs. Heinkel. He directed me and Dad to follow Mrs. Griffin, the housekeeper, up the grand stairway.

I said hello to Mrs. Griffin and introduced my parents to the housekeeper who had been with the Heinkel family since they were married.

She kissed me on each cheek saying, "You look beautiful, sweetheart. Mr. Jiff is one lucky man today. Now, you and your father will be coming down the rear balcony stairway into the garden. The Archbishop is waiting there to perform the ceremony. Please follow me."

The Archbishop, as in the Archbishop of the City of New Orleans? Oh my, I thought. His mother really went all out to shut my mother up over the not being married in church!

I looked over my shoulder and smiled at my mother who looked like she was in a trance. A trance of disbelief at my good fortune.

I could hear my dad asking Mrs. Griffin, "Did you

say the Archbishop is here to officiate?"

"Yes," she said. "Mr. Heinkel asked the Archbishop as a personal favor since your daughter couldn't have a church wedding during this trying time with Covid."

At the top of the stairs, I looked down and the butler was telling my mother, "Mrs. Alexander this is the groom's brother, Jay Heinkel, Esquire. He will escort you to your seat so that the wedding can commence."

I really thought someone was going to have to slap my mother and say, 'Snap out of it' to get her to move.

At the top of the stairs, Jiff's sister was waiting for us with a camera in her hand snapping photos. She had a lens long enough to stretch all the way down St. Charles Avenue from Canal Street to the river. She set her camera down on a nearby table and hugged me with both arms and gave me a kiss. "OMG! You are gorgeous. My brother is wildly lucky and happy. We are all thrilled that Jiff has found the perfect soulmate in you," she said. To my dad, "Hello, I'm Jiff's sister, and I'll be taking photos for the lovebirds. Nice to meet you. Call me Sis… everybody does."

My dad shook her hand. He didn't say anything, but he just nodded a lot and then turned away so neither of us could see he was getting emotional.

She continued, "Just ignore me once the ceremony starts. I'll stay out of the way, but I'd like to get some of you and your dad here. I'll run down the inside stairs and be out back to take some of you coming down.

Now, let me get a couple of you and your dad. You both look amazing." She was clicking away.

When Dad and I walked out onto the balcony overlooking the back of the Heinkels' home, I could see the garden was gloriously done in all white roses and orchids. Their pergola stood in the middle of the patio section of their yard away from the pool. It was covered in white roses for Jiff and me to stand in front of while the Archbishop stood under it. There were white flowers arrangements on the end of three rows of chairs. A white runner lead from the bottom of the grand curving outdoor stairway from the second-floor balcony where we stepped out, all the way to the flowered arch where the Archbishop was waiting. White rose petals were strewn along the path to my future husband.

"Boy, they sure went all out for a small wedding. I'm glad I wore a tux," Dad said. "Are you ready?" he asked me when Mrs. Griffin closed the door to the balcony behind us.

All his brothers were there with their wives. Jiff's sister, Ava and Suzanne were the only guests without a plus one.

My mother was being shown to the front row seat, second from the aisle I was about to walk down. The front row was for the parents of the bride and groom and the second row was for the rest of the family and friends. Some of the Heinkel's spilled over to sit in the third row on my side. My sister, Sherry and the twin she married sat in the first row with my mother. Ava and Suzanne were in the second row, and that was it for my side. The empty chair on the aisle was for my dad. There were six on my side and sixteen on the Heinkel side counting the Archbishop, Mrs. Griffin and the butler.

I just nodded. Seeing everything so beautifully done for me and Jiff had me fighting back tears. I did not want to cry. A red nose and red eyes in my wedding photos were not what I wanted to see years from now.

I heard soft music playing when we stepped out onto the rear balcony. At first, it had been a soft harp music playing until my dad and I were in position to come down the stairs. I saw Jiff's sister give a signal to someone, and then I heard the wedding march begin on a piano. When we came down the staircase, there, under the second-floor balcony was a trio, a baby grand piano and pianist, a harp and a flutist.

We said our vows in what felt like a dream, and I finally realized I was Mrs. Jiff Heinkel when the Archbishop said, "I now pronounce you husband and wife. You may now kiss your bride."

Everyone moved to the double parlor where I first met Jiff's parents. The waiters served everyone a glass of champagne on silver trays and Jiff's dad and brothers all took turns toasting us, the day and the family. My dad rallied and gave a respectable toast celebrating our big day. Thankfully, my mother kept her mouth shut.

Everything happened way too fast. After dinner we cut our five tier wedding cake. It was beautiful and more than I could have hoped for given the small ceremony. When we finished our cake, Felix came and advised Jiff it was time to leave for the airport. We started saying our goodbyes.

Walking down the grand entrance of the Heinkel home, the butler, the housekeeper and Jiff's mother all threw white rose petals mixed with a little rice on us. Mrs. Heinkel wanted grandkids.

"Where are we going? I didn't know airlines were flying passengers anywhere," I said to Jiff.

"We're not going on an airline. We're taking the company jet to Aruba for a few days," he said.

Just to make sure my mother heard, I kissed my dad goodbye and said it in his ear. He had a surprised, but happy face for me. He'd tell her later.

When we were alone on the private jet heading to Aruba I asked, "How did you get the Archbishop of New Orleans to perform our ceremony?" I asked.

"My dad and the Archbishop know each other from the prep school they both attended. My mother is on several boards that plan fund raisers for the Archdiocese, and she helps with the legalities placing adoptive children in homes for Catholic Charities. When your mother told my mother, she was concerned about us not being married in a Catholic Church, my dad asked the Archbishop to bring the church to us for the ceremony. He agreed.

"The only board my mother has ever been on was the ironing board." I said. "I won the lottery with my new mother-in-law. I'm sorry to tell you, but you got short-changed on yours."

We kissed while the airplane engine revved and prepared for takeoff.

THE END

Dear Reader:

Hello and thank you for reading my work. If you enjoyed this book, I'd love it if you would leave a review on Amazon. Reviews are vital to an author just as a good grade point average is crucial to a student. Your feedback would mean the world to me.

I'd also love to hear from you. Here is my Facebook author page and my email is ColleenMooneyAuthor@gmail.com.

Please join my website's Newsletter at www.colleenmooney.com. I hope you also follow me on BookBub. This way, you'll be the first to know about free giveaways, free books, sales or new books about to release! I hope you decide to stay in touch. Thanks, again for reading.

Colleen

You've finished. Before you go…

<u>Tweet/share that you finished this book</u>

Rate this book   Your Rating: _ _ _ _ _

Customers who bought this book also bought
Rescued By A Kiss
Dead and Breakfast
Drive Thru Murder
Death By Rum Balls
Dog Gone & Dead
Politicians, Potholes & Pralines
Fireworks, Forensics & Felonies
Voodoo, Victims & Vows
Croissants, Crimes & Canines
MORE TO COME BY THIS AUTHOR

RECIPES

French Quarter Beignets

Yields about 5-6 dozen

- 1 1/2 cups lukewarm water (115*F)
- 1/2 cup granulated sugar
- 2 envelopes active dry yeast
- 2 eggs, slightly beaten
- 1 1/4 teaspoons salt
- 1 cup evaporated milk
- 7 cups All Purpose Flour
- 3 teaspoons ground cinnamon
- 1/2 teaspoon freshly grated nutmeg
- 1/4 cup room temp. BUTTER, cut up into bits
- Nonstick spray
- Oil, for deep-frying, USE CLEAN, NOT REUSED OIL
- 3 cups confectioners' sugar

Directions

Mix slightly warm water, sugar, and yeast in a large bowl and let sit for 10 minutes to proof.

In another bowl, beat the eggs, salt and evaporated milk

together. Mix egg mixture into the yeast mixture. In a separate bowl, measure out the flour and whisk in the salt, cinnamon and nutmeg. Add 3 cups of the flour to the yeast mixture and stir to combine. Add the butter and continue to stir while adding another 3 cups flour. (Save remaining flour to dust the cutting surface.) Remove dough from the bowl, place onto a lightly floured surface and knead until smooth. Spray a large, clean bowl with nonstick spray or drizzle over a little vegetable oil to coat. Put dough into the bowl and cover with plastic wrap or a towel. Let rise in a warm place for at least 2 hours. Preheat oil in a deep fryer to 350 degrees F.

Add the confectioners' sugar to a paper or plastic bag or place in a large sieve over a large bowl and set aside.

Roll the dough out to about 1/4-inch thickness and cut into 2-inch squares. Deep-fry, flipping once or twice, until they become a golden color. After beignets are fried, drain them for a few seconds on paper towels, and then toss them into the bag of confectioners' sugar. Hold bag closed and shake to coat evenly. Or sieve the hot beignets with lots of confectioner's sugar. Serve immediately!!!!!!!!!!

WASHINGTON PIE

1/3 cup butter

1 cup sugar

2 eggs beaten

1 3/4 cups sifted flour

1/2 teaspoon salt

1/4 cup milk

1 teaspoon almond extract

Raspberry or apricot jam

Powdered sugar

1/3 teaspoon baking powder

Cream butter until soft and then beat in sugar gradually. Add eggs, well beaten. Combine sifted cake flour with baking powder and salt and sift again.

Combine almond extract and milk. Add dry ingredients and milk to first mixture alternating in small batches until all is combined.

Turn into two 6" greased layer cake tins and bake at 375 for about 25 minutes. Let cool or put in refrigerator. When cold, put together with jam and dust with powdered sugar.

This is NOT the Picou's Bakery Washington Pie. If you want to try to make the Picou Bakery one, I suggest you substitute the sifted flour for glazed donuts. Try to crumble them to make the right amount (1 3/4 cup). Their pies were incredibly dense and GOOD!

About the Author

Colleen Mooney is a two time USA Today and Wall Street Journal Best Selling Author. Book 6 in her series, Politicians, Potholes and Pralines was an Amazon Best Seller. Colleen was born and lived much of her life in New Orleans before her AT&T job moved her to multiple cities, but she always bounced back to New Orleans. She writes a cozy mystery series set in New Orleans called *The New Orleans Go Cup Chronicles.*

In January 2017 Colleen founded a Sisters in Crime chapter in New Orleans. The chapter holds monthly meetings with guest speakers from various law, legal or medical agencies to help chapter writers have a better understanding of how crimes are investigated or solved in order to improve our stories.

Colleen's other great loves, besides writing, is a breed rescue group, Schnauzer Rescue of Louisiana that she has been the Director of for 19 years and has placed over 375 abandoned or surrendered Schnauzers.

Colleen enjoys Scuba diving and Underwater photography, racing sailboats, driving a motorcycle, and snow skiing. Her interests have taken her to places all over the world. She says, "My mother said I was born with a suitcase in my hand!"

In New Orleans, she's been active in many Mardi

Gras Krewes, Super Krewes, and organizations and has belonged to the Krewe of Cork, Orpheus, Iris, Tucks, Joan of Arc and the Halloween Krewe of Boo. Colleen says she has never met a parade she didn't like.